OUTLAW BRAND

OUTLAW BRAND

William Vance

GUNSMOKE

First published in the US by Avalon Books

This hardback edition 2011
by AudioGO Ltd
by arrangement with
Golden West Literary Agency

ISBN 978 1 445 85686 5

British Library Cataloguing in Publication Data available.

Printed and bound in Great Britain by
MPG Books Group Limited

William E. Vance was the author of radio plays, articles, and, beginning in 1952 with *The Branded Lawman* published by Ace Books, of some twenty Western novels. Living for much of his life in Seattle, Washington, in the 1960s he began writing hardcover Western novels, most notably *Outlaw Brand* (Avalon, 1964) and *Tracker* (Avalon, 1964), as well as *Son of a Desperado* for Ace Books in 1966, one of his most notable works. There followed a decade in which he published no Western fiction, only to return, publishing what remain his most outstanding novels with Doubleday: *Drifter's Gold* (1979), *Death Stalks The Cheyenne Trail* (1980), and *Law And Outlaw* (1982), his final novel. "Sound characterization, careful attention to historical background, and a fine story sense were Vance's strong points as a novelist," Bill Pronzini pointed out in *Twentieth Century Western Writers* (St. James Press, 1991). "Vance's untimely death cut short a promising career which seemed to improve with every book, and his works are well worth reading by anyone interested in the traditional Western story."

CHAPTER ONE

The trail crews were gone and the town lay quiet in the sun. Town Constable Logan Marlowe stepped out of Charley Wang's with his toothpick at an angle that reached for the deep blue sky and surveyed Rawhide Street. He looked at Haymes with pleasure on this morning. He liked the town and the town liked him. The last trail crew had come and gone with a minimum of trouble, leaving behind a considerable portion of their pay and only one complaint from Dutch Annie, a relatively minor one; a cowhand had wandered into forbidden territory and kicked over a cherished potted plant.

Down by the livery a tawny cat stalked a black hen that unconcernedly scratched in the litter from the stable. Frank Dupre came from the Haymes House and sauntered across the street to the barber shop. You'd never know, Logan thought, that the man had had a run of bad luck with this last trail crew and lost over six thousand dollars. A gambler—at least a straight one—never knew for sure what the cards held; and Frank Dupre, Logan knew, was a straight one. That was the only kind he allowed in Haymes.

Logan Marlowe was a tall man in his thirties. He was wide-shouldered in a noticeable way, with the lean shanks of a rider and a brown, composed face that held little trace of his vagrant past. His steel-gray eyes were both wise and humorous and the tiny wrinkles at the corner betrayed the laughter that lay underneath.

Glenn Hutchins came from the bank and surveyed the street and nodded to Logan. "Heard anything else?" he asked worriedly, adjusting the black sleeve protectors he habitually wore on his skinny arms.

"So far as I know, she'll be in at nine-fifteen," Logan said, and pulled the big gold watch from his vest pocket and looked at it. "I checked with Clem just before breakfast. He said it was on time then."

Clem Shaker was the telegraph operator, station and freight agent.

Glenn Hutchins looked at his own watch. "Just thirty minutes away," he grunted. "Thought there'd be a lot of folks to see this new Wisdom come in."

"They're gathering," Logan said, nodding toward the cross street that led into the station. A fringe-top pulled by two high-stepping blacks was just turning into the cross street. Three gaudily dressed girls were sitting on the cushions. Swampy, Dutch Annie's handy man, was driving the rig.

Glen Hutchins grunted again and said nothing.

As if on signal, other people appeared on the street and headed for the depot. Curly Johnson came out of the livery and walked through the dust. He turned and picked up a cob and threw it at the stalking cat and said, "Scat!" The tawny cat gave up its stalking game and fled. The black hen scratched on, unruffled. Chet Morley carefully hung his leather apron on a post of the ramada and angled across the street after Curly. Slim Reed came down the steps of the Haymes House and mounted his horse to ride the short distance to the railroad station.

"Wonder what Slim's doing in town so early," Logan mused idly.

"He stayed here last night. He didn't do so bad with that trail crew, either."

Kirk Hutchins, Glenn's young son, came out of the door and stood behind his father. He said, "Good morning, Marshal."

Logan nodded and smiled at Kirk. He liked young Kirk, who'd recently returned from back East, where he'd been to school. The boy dressed here as he had back East, not even wearing boots, which most everyone else did. He was a well-setup young man with curly brown hair and bright blue eyes. He was nineteen years old and his smooth face was free of guile. He said, "If you're not going over to the station, I'd like to go, Pa."

Glenn Hutchins said irritably, "Me and you neither one got any business over there."

Kirk didn't say anything. He turned after a moment and went back into the bank.

Logan touched his hat and touched his gun and adjusted his belt. "Guess I'll walk over," he said.

"Expect any trouble?" Glenn asked.

Logan looked at him. "I still think Ben Wisdom got killed accidentally."

"He'd sure been laying it onto the Candlishes," Glenn said.

"I know that," Logan replied patiently. "But that doesn't spell nothing. Ben laid it on to whoever he thought was wrong. He gave me a bad time when I first took this job."

"That's right," Glenn admitted. "He did. But that's a horse of a different color. That Candlish bunch don't take to being whipped in the paper. And Ben was almighty good at it."

"He was," Logan said.

"Bring that woman over here as soon as she gets in," Glenn said. "I want to find out what she plans to do."

"She's anything like her brother," Logan said, "I might have trouble bringing her anywhere. Ben had a mind of his own."

"Can't imagine Ben Wisdom having a sister," Glenn said. "Probably a dried-up old maid whose disposition would sour a wild cow's milk."

"We'll see." Logan moved on across the street.

He was surprised at the number of people gathered on the station platform. He was even more surprised to see Kirk Hutchins standing alone at the end, near where Dutch Annie's surrey had stopped. Swampy was standing at the heads of the horses, holding to their bridle reins, to keep them from bolting when the train came in. The girls were quiet and composed, and Logan saw that the one called Mary and Kirk Hutchins were looking at each other in a manner that betokened more than casual interest. Logan whistled a tuneless note and moved farther down the platform. A look at Kirk made him wince inwardly and, again gauging the looks between the two, he expelled his breath. Glenn wouldn't like that.

A train whistled in the distance and Logan looked at his watch again; the train was now seven minutes late. It whistled into the station a few minutes later with the bell ringing and screeched to a jerking halt. No one alighted from the train except the conductor, and he walked rapidly down the splintered platform toward the station, the long black coattails of his Prince Albert streaming. Clem Shaker came to meet him. They talked for a few minutes while Logan scanned the crowd to see if any of the Candlish brothers had ridden in to meet the train. He didn't see one single Candlish.

Clem Shaker came running across the platform and hauled up suddenly, waving to Logan. Logan walked down the cinders and stepped up on the platform, facing Clem Shaker. The conductor was now entering the station and the door closed on him.

"What's up?" Logan asked.

"The train was stopped," Clem Shaker said. "A couple of hardcase holdup jaspers searched the train for that Wisdom woman."

"Where is she?"

Clem jerked his head. "Still on the train. Conductor wants to talk to you."

Logan walked swiftly toward the station. At the door he stopped short. He looked again and saw the Candlish twins sitting their horses beyond the crowd. Slender, dark men, they lounged in the saddle, talking back and forth, and grinning widely. Logan jerked open the door and went in.

The conductor was a new man. He mopped his brow with a red bandanna and stowed it back in the hip pocket of his shiny blue pants. "You the marshal?" he asked.

"Town constable," Logan said briefly.

"Afraid to take Miss Wisdom off the train without an escort," the conductor said. "Never seen the like. These two had rocks piled on the track. When we stopped they got the engineer and marched him ahead of them and into the passenger cars. Wasn't looking for nobody but Miss Wisdom. I told them she wasn't on my train. They went through the car and asked every woman on it some questions. But they couldn't take them all. So they left."

"Where's the woman?"

"Still on the train."

"All right, let's go get her. She does want to stay here until her business is finished, doesn't she?"

The conductor, a red-faced man with a black handlebar mustache nodded. "She does." He headed for the door and Logan followed.

He made a way through the crowd and stepped

up into the vestibule of the coach and ducked his head and went into the car. The passengers were all standing, looking out the window. They stopped looking and swung around as the tall man came into the car.

The conductor edged around Logan and went back and leaned over the girl in the third seat and said something to her.

She raised her head and looked directly at Logan. Her eyes were a steady brown and her gaze was direct. She was young and smooth-skinned and as she stood up smoothing out her gray skirt, Logan saw that she was well-formed, with straight shoulders, a full bosom and nice hips. A tiny, fur-trimmed vest that matched her skirt accented the slimness of her waist. She stepped out gracefully and came forward to stand before Logan, looking up at him.

A tiny electric tremor ran through him as he looked into her brown eyes. He said, "I don't think you've got a thing to worry about here."

"No," she said. "I guess not. I'm Kathleen Wisdom." She put out her hand.

He accepted her handshake and found her hand warm and firm. "I'm Logan Marlowe," he said. "Town constable."

She stepped past him and went down the steps as Logan leaned down with his hand under her arm. She waited, glancing at the crowd with interest animating her face. He saw that her complexion was not dark, not light, but somewhere between an olive color. Her cheeks held a bright spot of red in each of them, but it seemed natural to him. Her lips were pink and slightly parted, showing even white teeth. With a slight shock Logan found himself comparing her to Gail Howard. He felt a flush of heat rise to his neck and he said, "Let's go right over to the bank. Mr. Hutchins wants to see you right away."

She walked beside him through the crowd and as they broke beyond the far reaches Logan found two horsemen barring his way. He stopped and then stepped ahead of the girl and stared up into the dark, restless eyes of Faron Candlish—or was it Aaron? He saw the tiny scar showing through the dark bristles on the man's chin and knew it was Aaron.

"Back up, Aaron," he said in a quiet voice.

"Sure, Marshal," Aaron said, showing his sharp incisors in a humorless grin. "Just wanted to get a look at Ben's sister."

"An' tell her to get her inheritance and get out of town," Faron said from behind Aaron.

The crowd drew back and some of them leaped up on the platform so they could see better. Others who could not see were shouting out from the outer fringes, wanting to know what was going on.

Logan took another step to shield the girl more completely, and saw that she was taking this all in with an air of interest rather than concern. He put his hand on the bit ring of Aaron's horse and pushed; the animal reared. Logan stepped back to the girl and said, to both of them, "Ride out right now, boys."

Faron stopped the quick reply on his lips as Aaron

held up his hand with an easy grin. "All right," Aaron drawled with excessive politeness. "Gotta have a partner you wanta dance. Just like you say, Marshal, we're ridin' out."

The two turned their mounts and headed toward the cattle pens to the north of town.

Kathleen Wisdom looked after them. She sensed an underlying current of violence that puzzled her. She'd watched the law officer carefully and saw that he was coldly controlled all the time, that he let the men know just how far they could go. She sensed a hard core in the big man.

As for Logan he watched them for a moment and then glanced at her, a question in his eyes.

She nodded, not thinking it strange that she knew he was asking her to go. "I'd like to look at the shop, first," she said. "If you don't mind."

"I don't mind, but Mr. Hutchins is waiting for you."

"He has waited for two weeks," she said smilingly. "A little longer won't hurt him. Who were those two men?"

"Aaron and Faron Candlish."

"That doesn't mean much," she said as they walked slowly toward Rawhide Street. "Are they the men Ben wrote up in the paper?"

"Part of them," Logan said. "There's four brothers—Jeb, the twins, and Duke, the youngest. They're tough customers."

"Did they kill Ben?"

"I don't think so," Logan said gently.

"You mean you can't prove they did or didn't?"

"No, I can't prove anything." He stopped in front of the *Courier* office. "This is it."

She looked at the dusty windows, and stepping closer peered through them, and then turning back to him with a wry smile said, "I can't see a thing through the window. Can we go in?"

"Mr. Huchins has the key," Logan said.

She glanced around and saw that the crowd had straggled back from the railroad station and was strung out along the street in little groups and she must have realized that she was the subject of many conversations. She asked, "Why are they so interested in me?"

"You're Ben's sister. He was quite a controversial figure around here."

"Why?" She studied him for a moment and added, "I didn't know my brother very well, Mr. Marlowe. He left home when I was very small. I was three, I think."

He thought of her as a three-year-old and couldn't make the transformation in his mind. She was so much alive at her present age. "The country. All on this side of the canyon is prosperous ranchers. The grass is good and the cattle market is good. Ranchers like Giff Howard are doing very well. They've had some lean years, but that's all behind. They're wealthy men, most of them."

"That should be good for the town."

"Yes. But across the canyon there isn't much. It has little graze, little water, mostly running to cactus, lava, sand and scorpions. The men who live over there are poor as pack rats. They've got hungry eyes on this side of the canyon."

"That makes the rich ones nervous?" she smiled.

He nodded. "That's about it. Here comes Mr. Hutchins now."

Glenn Hutchins must have watched them from the bank window and become impatient. He walked his straight-legged walk directly toward them and as he neared them he smiled at Kathleen Wisdom and took her outstretched hand.

"Mighty nice to meet you, Miss Wisdom," he said. "Shall we walk back to the bank?"

"If you have the key, I'd like to see the shop," she said.

He was irritated, but he took the bunch of keys from his belt and sorted them one by one until he found the right one. He opened the door and stood back, saying, "It's just like Ben left it."

She stepped through the door and looked at the disordered shop. A chair was lying on its side beside the desk. The desk drawers were opened and papers scattered on the floor. All the pigeonholes had been emptied; their contents littered the desk top and had spilled off on the dirty floor. There was a smell of ink and oily machinery in the air. A fly buzzed heavily against the dusty windowpane.

"Was he—did it happen in here?"

"No, ma'am," Logan said. "Right outside the door. He had just locked up. He had the key in his hand when I found him."

"He wouldn't lock up on a mess like this, would he?"

"I don't know," Logan said.

"Sure he would," Hutchins said. "Ben was a good man, but one of the untidiest I ever knew."

Kathleen Wisdom looked from Logan to Hutchins and said, "Shall we go to the bank now, Mr. Hutchins?" She glanced at Logan. "Would you come, too, please?"

"That won't . . ." Hutchins began, and then stopped abruptly. "All right, let's go."

In the bank, a dark, musty building that held a wire-cage and seemed to surround a big, double-doored wall safe, Hutchins drew up a chair for the girl, and motioned for Logan to be seated. He drew a thick envelope from a pigeonhole and unsnapped the rubber band that encircled it.

"Ben owed me seven hundred dollars on the building and equipment," he said. "Here's the mortgage note and all the papers. Now, if you want me to, I can simply sell it, get enough to pay off the mortgage, and send the balance to you."

The girl didn't reply. She was busy going through the papers and quickly scanning them and laying them aside. When she had finished, she looked at Hutchins and said crisply, "I do not wish to sell the *Courier*, Mr. Hutchins, I intend to operate it."

Glenn Hutchins stared at her as though he thought she'd lost her mind. "You? You're going to run a newspaper?"

She flushed and nodded.

"Well, that's fine," Hutchins said sarcastically. "The only thing I'm worried about is the bank's money. There's a little matter of seven hundred dollars and I don't think I could in good conscience give you the same terms I gave Ben. After all, he was an experienced newspaper editor and printer."

She was fumbling in her purse. She came out with an envelope that she extended to Hutchins. "This is a letter of credit from my bank in St. Louis," she said. "I will take up the note as soon as funds can be transferred."

Hutchins looked at the envelope and took it and slowly opened it. He read the contents and put it back into the envelope, compressing his lips into a thin line. "All right," he said. "If you want to run the paper, that's your funeral."

Kathleen Wisdom looked quickly at Logan. "Then running a newspaper in Haymes is a dangerous occupation."

"Glenn said that as a figure of speech," Logan said, looking at Hutchins. "Isn't that right, Glenn?"

Hutchins nodded almost imperceptibly. "Kirk," he said. "Kirk, come here."

Kirk hastily left his stool in the cage and came around to stand beside his father. Glenn gave him the letter of credit and said, "See that the transfer is made, Kirk. Get the papers all ready and just as soon as the funds arrive have Miss Wisdom come in and sign and take over the *Courier*, lock, stock and barrel."

"Yes, sir, Pa," Kirk said, and took the papers and went back to his cage.

Kathleen Wisdom stood up and extended her hand to Hutchins. "Thank you for your kindness, sir," she said quietly. She looked at Logan and they went out together.

Back at the *Courier* office, Logan tried to warn her. "Women don't figure much in the business world around here," he said. "Glenn Hutchins is a good man. He just doesn't believe a woman can successfully operate any kind of business."

"What do you think?" she asked.

He shrugged and changed the subject. "What did the men look like who tried to take you off the train?"

She laughed without coyness. "You're dodging the question, but I'll let you off for now." Her forehead wrinkled. "They wore masks. But one was tall and dark and the other short and reddish."

"The tall, dark one—was he heavy, very heavy?"

She shook her head. "No, I don't think so. His tallness was noticeable, but he wasn't fat. I could see the outline of a beard through the mask. So he had a black beard."

"Jeb Candlish has a black beard," Logan said thoughtfully, "but he's heavy as well as tall. You see a bear walking, that's Jeb."

"The Candlishes are the poor people across the canyon?" she asked.

Logan nodded. "People think they're pretty rough

characters. Ben was just beginning to give them hell in his newspaper when he got killed."

She said, "I'm a little mixed up, Mr. Marlowe. You say Ben got killed. Then when we were walking over here you said you didn't think the Candlish men killed him. What do you think?"

"A trail crew was in town," Logan said. "They can get pretty rough just having normal fun. I think some trailhand was shooting off his gun and accidentally killed Ben."

She looked past him with thoughtful eyes, then she opened her purse and took a letter out and offered it to him. "That's Ben's last letter," she said. "Read it, Marshal."

He opened the letter and saw the familiar scrawl of Ben Wisdom on the sheet of rough newsprint. He read:

Dear Kathy: Thanks for the newspaper clippings. You know this is the first word we've had of General Grant's death, but that's only natural as old Clem Shaker was in the rebel army and if he copied anything on the telegraph about U. S. Grant it would never get past his office door. Thanks anyway, and if you keep on sending them, it'll spice up the newspaper a lot.

Not that it needs spicing up. I've run into something here that'll make the whole county sit up and take notice. Trouble is, I don't just know how to handle it because it means making a hard decision and I'm not good at that.

Seems funny, really, that our first newspaper in these United States was started just about one hundred years ago this month. The art and craft has flourished, but men haven't changed any. The man in the newspaper business has it hard trying to figure what's right and what's wrong so he can help his readers accordingly. Well, I'll try, but anything can happen and likely will. This is a situation where a man can get himself killed in this violent country.

Love,
Ben

Logan looked up and found the girl watching him. He said, "Ben had uncovered something that added up to trouble. What was it?"

"All the way out here," she said steadily, "I thought I could just ask and find out."

"I don't know," Logan said.

"How can we find out?"

He shook his head. "I'll have to check around and see what I can dig up."

"What can I do to help?" she asked eagerly.

"Nothing right now. But I can do something for you—help you find a place to live."

"Would you?"

"It's a problem. There's the hotel and that's about all."

"Where do you live?"

He grinned. "In a boardinghouse for men only."

"That wouldn't do for me, then," she said, smiling. "I guess it'll have to be the hotel."

"It's a pretty nice hotel," he said, "for this part of the country," and was gratified that she didn't tell him that wasn't saying much.

He saw Kathleen Wisdom to the hotel and then went out on the street and tramped down the boards toward his own office.

Gail Howard was wrapping the reins around her buggy whip and he put his hand up and she stepped to the ground. She was a tall, imperious girl with bright golden hair and deep blue eyes. She wore the latest fashions and was arbiter of society, such as it was, in Haymes. She said lightly, "What's all the fuss about, Marshal?"

"Ben's sister just got in," he said. "Everybody in town turned out to meet her at the station."

"You mean, why wasn't I there?" she asked laughingly. "I've got better things to do, Logan. I did hear something about a fight, though."

"The Candlish twins," Logan said. "Wasn't nothing at all."

She looked sharply at him, seeing the spark in his eyes. "Nothing, Logan?" She touched his cheek lightly. "What does she look like?"

"Well. She's not as tall as you. Kind of plain and—and—well, I just don't know."

Kathleen Wisdom chose that moment to come out of the Haymes House and turned down the street. She passed them, nodding to Logan, and went on, after a brief glance at Gail Howard.

"Plain, did you say, Logan?" Gail asked, squeezing his arm. "I'd better have your eyes examined. You could get yourself in trouble running into a bluff or something."

But inwardly, she felt a deep satisfaction.

CHAPTER TWO

In the days that passed, Logan saw Kathleen Wisdom only from a distance. He saw her as she left the hotel early in the morning, going to the newspaper office. Sometimes he saw her briefly during the day, as she walked to the railroad station, to the post office, or to the bank. He saw her when he made his rounds in late evening and sometimes at night he'd catch a glimpse of her in the hotel lobby. She was rapidly becoming the scandal of the proper wives in town. Some said she even played poker and someone else enlarged on that by saying if she played poker she drank whisky.

She did play poker, Logan knew. He talked to Doc Custis and the little chunky physician who doctored the whole country, including horses and steers, chuckled. "Play poker? That gal's the best dad-burned poker player I've run into around here. Been trying to figger out how I can get her to use my money and split with me after buckin' Frank Dupre's game at the Golden Slipper."

Logan felt drawn to Kathleen despite the fact that he and Gail Howard were engaged to be married. It was for this very reason that he avoided Kathleen when possible. It wasn't always possible, however, and some nights when she worked late he'd walk with her from the *Courier* office to the hotel. Walking beside her with his arm brushing hers, with the spicy odor of her perfume in his nostrils, he would feel strangely guilty.

One night, as if sensing it, she looked up at him and said, "Miss Howard is a very pretty girl."

That dispelled some of his guilt. He agreed in his taciturn way that Miss Howard was pretty. But he didn't want to talk about Gail.

"The first paper you put out. It's real good," he said. And it was, too. She had a sense of humor that Ben hadn't had, and it showed in the weekly newspaper. Most of the people Logan had talked to about it had commented favorably on it.

"Why, thank you, Logan," she said. She laughed. "You may be surprised, but I died several times before that first issue."

"Where'd you learn newspaper business?"

"I didn't," she said. "Merl Young gives me much more help than he ever gave Ben."

"When he's sober, maybe."

Merl Young was the alcoholic printer who'd worked on the *Courier* for years. He was as unpredictable as the winds that blew ceaselessly across Snaketrack.

"Merl's all right," she defended him. "He does like

the bottle, but then . . ." She cut off her words abruptly and said, "People are just too darn critical."

"Always—of everybody else, except me and you." Logan grinned.

She laughed and he liked the sound of it, a real laugh coming right out of her as though she meant it.

They reached the hotel and she stopped, looking up at him. "Have you found out anything about what Ben mentioned in his letter?"

"I sure haven't. I asked most people who knew Ben and might have some idea. But nobody has even a guess, not even Merl, who worked with him every day he was sober."

"Nothing has happened so far," she said seriously. "I was a little nervous at first. I do often wonder what Ben knew."

"I couldn't scare up a single good guess," Logan said.

She looked away from him. "The mayor, the judge, Doc Custis and I are having a little poker game tonight. Care to join us?"

He said soberly, "Not tonight; maybe some other time."

"Good night, Logan."

He watched her walk into the hotel and then he turned toward his own office. Someone was in there, he could see as he approached. He looked through the window and saw Sheriff Jones and his deputy, Al Macklin.

Wondering, he pushed open the door and went in, hanging his hat on the rack beside the door.

Sheriff Jerico Jones was ancient. His face was lined, and brown as a nut, but his blue eyes were sharp and missed nothing. He was inclined to be forgetful in his old age and had a certain childishness at times. His deputy, Al Macklin, was a brooding, narrow-faced, dark man, with an explosive temper.

"Two cowboys rode through today," Jones began without preliminaries. "Claimed somebody shot at 'em with a rifle as they crossed Snaketrack."

"Anybody get hurt?" Logan asked, nodding to the still silent Macklin.

Jerico shook his snow-white head. "Me and Al rode out. Jeb met us just across the bridge. Said Snaketrack range was closed. Didn't aim to hurt nobody but they didn't want trespassers ridin' through."

"Sounds tame for Jeb," Logan said.

Jerico shook his head again. "Got me stumped. Nobody in their right mind would ride through Snaketrack nohow. But a stranger wouldn't know."

"He has a right to post his property," Logan said.

"Well, I thought I'd let you know," Jerico said, rising painfully and moving toward the door. He paused there, looking at Logan. "Saw Giff today. He wants us all out tomorrow. To talk about next election."

Logan smiled at that. "He wants me to run for sheriff."

"Me, too," Jerico said. "I'm not standing again. Too old, for one thing."

"Why doesn't Al here take the job?"

Deputy Al Macklin shot him a swift look. "Glad

you asked that," he said sourly. "Up to now ain't nobody asked me."

"Well, now, Logan," Jerico said testily, "most people we talked to lean toward you. Don't you want it?"

"I've got two sections on the good side of the canyon," Logan said good-naturedly. "I'd like to see it stocked with blooded beef and that's about the extent of how far ahead I'm looking."

"Now me, I'd just be interested in being a good lawman," Macklin said. "But can't get nobody to listen. Not to me, nohow."

"You'll be considered when time comes," Jerico said shortly. "Come on, let's go. These long rides stove me in somethin' terrible."

Sitting there alone, after the two left, Logan let his thoughts idle the whole range, from what he knew to what he suspected. He held nothing back, not even his own past which had come out to haunt him less and less as time went on.

He was still not convinced that Ben Wisdom had been deliberately killed. But knowing Ben as he had, he knew the man was next to some discovery or had made an actual discovery that could be explosive. Could that unknown be connected with Snaketrack? He considered the possibility in minute detail. Snaketrack was a wild and rugged country, not fit to raise cattle or maybe not even a goat. The only reason the Candlishes settled there was simple; there was just no other place to go. The Candlish family certainly had not won any amount of wealth from that poor country. The money they spent, most people figured, came from outright thievery or helping some outlaw on the dodge; or even pointing out to rustler drifters where they might pick up a herd of cattle or horses, and then sharing with them. That was speculation, he knew. Nothing had ever been proved against the Candlish family. The Candlishes painted themselves as unfortunates who survived by being tougher than the tough country in which they lived. They were poor, but they asked nothing of any man but to be left alone.

Logan stirred restlessly. This idle conjecture was getting him nowhere. He was vexed at himself for not being able to make up his own mind about the Candlish brothers. They were not a likeable bunch, not that he'd ever been able to discover. All of them carried a chip on their shoulders, but that could come from living in perpetual hard times.

And now they'd closed Snaketrack to all outsiders. He wondered for a long, silent period what that could mean. And when nothing came to him from the inner recesses of his mind, he got his hat, closed the office door and went across town to Allie Adamson's rooming house on Cheyenne.

Anyway, he told himself, as he walked through the starlit night, *what happens outside Haymes doesn't concern me.* But somehow that reassurance fell very flat, as though he didn't really believe it himself.

CHAPTER THREE

Town Constable Logan Marlow came out of the cool mustiness of Curly Johnson's Livery as the lone horseman went past. The midday sun shone hot on a deserted street. Logan hauled up abruptly, his tall, rangy body tensing. Another rider drifted in from the other end of the street. The two men came together in front of the bank.

While Logan watched they got out of their saddles and looked around carefully before wrapping reins around the hitching rack. This done, they hitched their belts and moved toward the open door of the bank. Hutchins kept the doors wide on warm days.

The two of them approaching from opposite ends of town meant nothing to Logan. Their looks and actions told him more—the manner in which they moved, touching their holstered guns from time to time. Logan walked toward the bank, keeping close to the buildings.

He could smell trouble because he had lived with

it most of his life. The cut of these two men was as familiar to him as the black-handled gun that swung close to his hand. He looked toward the sheriff's office and saw he could expect no help there; the rack was empty, indicating that both Jerico and Al were gone.

A shot broke the stillness of the town. A short man ran out of the bank and unsnagged both horses in one easy motion. The other man followed, walking backward, holding his gun out in front of his body.

Logan had his own gun out and he called. The short man cast one swift look at Logan and yelled and got on his horse in one flying leap. The man with the gun triggered a shot as he turned his wild face toward Logan. Logan fired. The man wheeled away, his knees buckling crazily, and he fell sideways, half on the plank walk and half off, his shoulder and head raising a tiny cloud of dust.

The empty street was suddenly alive. Men ejected from the buildings as Logan approached the fallen outlaw, hoping he wouldn't know the man.

He didn't; the man was a stranger. Logan stood staring down at the gaunt, unshaven face, thinking, *That could have been me just as well as him.*

He knelt beside the man and removed the gun from the dirt-grained fingers, He examined the well-kept pistol, noting the trigger had been removed and the worn spot on the hammer. A gun thumber, or maybe a fanner. He automatically glanced at the outer edge of the man's left hand and saw the bump of callused flesh, indisputable proof of a gun fanner.

Doc Custis hurried up, panting with haste. "Hit bad?" he asked. A smallish, curly-haired man, he ran mostly to pink skin and paunch.

Logan rose to his tall height, towering over the short doctor. "Dead," he said. He leaned down and yanked the brown paper bag from inside the dead man's shirt. He looked inside the sack as Hutchins stepped outside the bank door, hesitantly and warily looked up and down the street. Seeing nothing threatening, he hurried toward the group.

There was two of them," Glenn Hutchins said. "What about the other one, Logan?"

"Rode out fast," Logan said briefly. He passed the brown paper sack to the banker. "This yours, I reckon."

The crowd had gathered quickly. They were quiet, except for low-voiced conjectures. Hutchins accepted the sack. He was a nervous man, fidgety and unsettled most of the time. He said, "Guess those two didn't know we got Logan Marlowe for town marshal."

Kathleen Wisdom edged through the crowd and stepped up and touched his arm. Her smile died instantly when she saw the man on the ground, his blood spreading in the dust around his head.

Logan watched her as she looked at the dead man and then turned her wide brown eyes on him, her hands clasped tightly together. "You're all right," she said, visibly paler. "I heard shooting."

"One of them fired to scare me," Hutchins said. "It did, all rightie."

Someone laughed and Logan saw Kathleen Wisdom wince.

There was other talk, argument about how many shots were fired. Logan only heard it as a distant sound.

"You take care of this, Doc," Logan told Custis, who was also Haymes' coroner and undertaker. "I'll ride on out and see if I can cut sign on the one that got away."

Several men eagerly offered to go with him. He refused without curtness. Hunting men was a very specialized kind of hunting. Experience had taught Logan to leave the eager but hotblooded ones behind.

He left them there staring at the dead man in morbid fascination and no one spoke to him as he walked toward the livery.

Kathleen Wisdom followed him and caught up with him by hurrying. "First holdup since the night you came to town," she said.

He glanced briefly at her. "You've been doing some studyin'," he said.

She nodded, wrinkling her forehead seriously. "That was a year ago, Logan. According to Ben's back issues, Haymes has been a peaceful town since."

He said shortly, "Guess that's why they hired me."

She stopped at the entrance to the barn and he looked at her again, seeing the perplexed forehead as she looked steadily at him. "It's hard to believe," she said. "One moment he was a living, breathing human being—and the next . . ."

"I don't like to think about it," he said harshly, and moved on into the livery stable.

He saddled his claybank and Kathleen was gone when he rode out the open door, ducking his head and then straightening in his saddle. There was still an empty hitch rack in front of Jerico's office as he rode out of town at a slow, mile-eating lope.

The riding and looking gradually wore down the knot in his belly. He kept thinking, *Glad I didn't know him.* He wondered how long it would be before someone rode into Haymes he did know. Haymes was a cattle town on the railroad, a shipping point for ranchers both north and south. It'd only be a matter of time until some of his old cahooters drifted through. He saw strangers every week, riding in and riding out. This was a country on the move and people didn't ask too many questions of anyone.

The deep hoofprints of a hard-running horse lightened two miles outside town and Logan nodded knowingly, his thoughts flashing back to then and now, out of his own experience. The bandit had slackened up from the hard run he'd taken out of town. The breed all conserved their horses as he well knew. Average-sized man, Logan thought, of thrifty movement and vaguely familiar. But then the dead man had seemed familiar, too. The men of that stripe all seemed to run to the same pattern, somehow.

Guess maybe, he thought, *I wasn't with 'em long enough to get it.*

In the dazzling bright distance between Logan and the dark of the mountains, the land lay quiet and gray. The wind moved with its unceasing push. Nothing moved until three riders drifted out from a distant draw, small in the long distance. He went on without slackening his pace because of the deep canyon that separated him from the riders. He followed the trail at a trot, the claybank patient and willing.

It was funny in a way, Logan thought, riding on the trail of an outlaw who'd tried to rob the Bank of Haymes. He'd known what it was like to ride into a town intent on taking a whack at the bank. Banks were rich and were legitimate prey. They robbed legally, whereas a man with a gun had more basic honesty, for he stacked himself up against big odds in a wild gamble. That was the way the Wild Bunch told it. He'd rode with them quite a piece.

But he'd never settled it in his own mind. He was a man who liked the other side of the hill and the new towns, and Haymes had been a new one just little more than a year ago. Haymes had held him, why he couldn't say.

The town had been wild, too. He'd bought himself a job with his gun that first day in town, when the scene of today was repeated as he tied his horse in front of Mitch Clagg's Golden Slipper. There had been two of them, then, and they had mistaken him for the town lawman and started shooting first.

It was a case of kill or be killed. When the smoke

cleared there were two dead bank robbers and Logan Marlowe was the local hero for a time. He'd worked briefly for Curly Johnson and then the town fathers offered him the job of town constable. This was how Logan Marlowe, who'd gone under the name of Joe Curran when he rode with the Wild Bunch, returned to respectability and the right side of the law. Now, he was accepted and respected by all. Even engaged to be married to the daughter of one of the country's big cattlemen.

He pulled up shortly at the sounds ahead and urged the claybank into the shelter of a cluster of gray rocks. He eased his Colt out of the holster and waited.

A group of three riders came into view and they hauled up short when they saw him there. The man in the lead, one of the Candlish twins—which one, Logan didn't know at first—spoke: "Lookin' for somebody, Constable?"

The three Candlish brothers rode forward as Logan holstered his gun. "Bank robber. One got away."

"An' the other one?" It was Aaron, Logan knew, by the scar almost concealed by the stubble of dark whiskers.

"He got shot," Logan said briefly.

There was a long silence and then Aaron said, "Just like them two a year ago, hey?"

Logan nodded. "How're things on Snaketrack?"

Aaron moved his shoulders. "Like same."

"How come you're so far south?"

"We'd druther ride forty miles than pay Hy Kelly

two bits to cross his damn bridge," Aaron said bluntly.

"You didn't see anyone along your way?" Logan nodded in the direction the Candlish brothers had come from. His horse moved nervously and Logan sensed that the smell of the brothers, rank and unwashed, was disturbing, even more than the odor disturbed him.

"We wouldn't tell you we did," Faron said.

"You keep shut, Faron," Aaron said. He swung back to Logan. "No, we ain't seen nothin', Constable. Not since leaving the Snake."

Logan wanted to ask them about their firing on trespassers, but he didn't want to get into an argument that would delay him. He waved his hand briefly and urged the claybank into motion. He glanced over his shoulder a few moments later and saw the Candlish brothers still sitting their horses, staring after him. He wondered about the oldest brother, Jeb, the mainspring of the unsavory outfit.

The Candlish brothers ruled Snaketrack country, the rough, rocky draw-crossed country west and south of Haymes. It was a lonely and remote area and the Candlishes were as tough as the country itself. Old Bramer Candlish had told them time and time again, "They don't want us here. Land ain't worth a damn but they still don't want us in here. You got to fight 'em all, every damn one of them."

Jeb Candlish, the old brother, ruled them all with an iron hand since Bramer's death. The other three, Aaron and Faron the twins, and Duke, still the baby at twenty-one, were all cut from the same cloth as Jeb. According to the town people, they were mean, sly, and not against rustling cows, stealing horses or harboring a man on the run. Snaketrack was unhealthy country for a lone rider who might happen in, the local gossip said. More than one thoughtless cowboy had rode into Snaketrack and was never heard of again.

When Logan disappeared over a rise, Faron said, "Damn law. Reckon he'll follow that track?"

"Hell, no," Aaron answered, grinning broadly. "More likely that redheaded feller won't even find the home place."

"Jeb'll skin you for sending him in," Duke said, looking balefully at Aaron. "He'll take off your hide."

"Maybe," Aaron said. "Ol' Jeb's gonna have his hands full o' that other stuff. He ain't gonna give me no trouble for a spell."

"You hope," Faron grunted. "Let's get movin'."

Duke was grinning now, a meanly joyous grin. "Can't wait to see how them high and mighty codgers in Haymes gonna take it."

"Fireworks, that's what," Aaron grunted, and spurred his horse. "Let's get."

When Logan looked again, the Candlish brothers had disappeared. He rubbed his chin, thinking of their dislike for riding in the open. They hung to draws, didn't skyline themselves, and generally acted like an Indian on the prowl.

Deep in his thoughts, he lost the trail on the rocky

bench, below the mountains. Patiently, he back-tracked, leaning from the saddle, looking at the rock-littered ground that went by. He rode almost back to the scraggly timber and the sun was westering when he found the tracks again. He stepped down and squatted on his hunkers, studying the imprint, trying to match it from memory with the ones he knew. They were the right prints, he decided and he stood and stretched and then climbed to the saddle, turning upgrade again.

The tracks ran out again and he looked at the sun and the distant smoke that marked Haymes and he turned back, toward the town.

A vague feeling of unrest was unsettling and irritating. A distant light flamed for a moment and died away. A rider lighting a cigarette as his horse drifted along. Logan had another flash of premonition and he touched the claybank into a trot as though he'd leave it behind.

CHAPTER FOUR

Back in town, Logan made his rounds as night came on with its lamplighting activity to break the after-supper lull. He kept the tired claybank at an easy trot that covered the town quick and thorough. Afterward, he left the horse at Curly Johnson's and went down the street with an easy stride, relaxed, the tensions gone. He rattled the bank door.

The door was locked and the town was clean and quiet. He stood there for a moment, a big man, easy on his feet, thinking that no matter how fast a man traveled, it wasn't fast enough to run away from his past.

He went on down the street as the pianola in the Golden Slipper started up, a tinkling tune that started Logan to humming under his breath. In the yellow light from behind the dusty window of the newspaper, he stopped, looking beyond the window. The place went dark as he stood there and in a moment the door opened and Kathleen came out. She was busy with the lock when he moved close and scratched a match alight.

She looked up, startled for a moment, and then she smiled. "Good evening, Logan," she said. "Thanks." She snapped the big lock shut.

Logan tossed the match away and stepped close to her and rattled the door. He could see the white flash of her teeth in the darkness.

"You don't take chances, do you, Logan?"

"Is that bad?" he asked her.

She didn't answer at once and then, "The other bandit—he got away?"

"Lost him up around Red Creek," he said.

"I'm sorry."

"Can't win 'em all," Logan answered, and moved restlessly.

"This won't hurt you a bit if you decide to run for sheriff."

"How'd you know about that?" he asked, surprised.

"Most everybody does," she answered, and her white teeth flashed again in the darkness. "I hope you win, Logan—if you make the race."

"Thanks," he said dryly.

"Don't thank me," she said tartly. "I haven't made up my mind about supporting anyone—newspaper support, I mean. I'm just beginning to realize what Ben was up against. The decisions—am I right or am I wrong?—and how do we learn the truth, the real truth."

He was silent, waiting for her to run on because he knew she had something else to say.

"The Candlish brothers are in town."

"I passed them up on the bench," he said, moving again, shifting from one foot to the other.

"Don't let me keep you," she said in a cross voice.

"I'm late now," he said apologetically. "Meeting." For some reason he felt compelled to add, "Business meeting. Why isn't Merl here when you work late? Never know who might drop in on a woman all alone."

He liked the sound of her laughter and his conscience twinged when he thought of Gail suddenly. He wondered why he'd never particularly noticed Gail's laughter.

"That might've been true before you became marshal," she said. "Now, it isn't."

"Constable," he corrected. "Let me walk to the hotel with you."

"You're late now," she said. "You can't keep Gail—or Mr. Howard—waiting."

He watched her as she moved down the street. And even in the darkness she was cloaked with a mysterious loveliness. He sighed, wondering.

"Logan." Her voice came out of the dark. "What about Al Macklin?"

"I don't know," he said. "I hadn't thought about it."

"You'd better," she warned. "He thinks he's set for the job."

He didn't answer that, but it came to him in a flash that this must be the truth. She came in daily contact with the town fathers and she knew sensibly, what was going on.

"Good night, Logan." She moved on.

He stood there, his mind troubled, because there were so many reasons why he should not run for sheriff. It would be difficult, if not impossible, to turn Giff Howard down. And it wasn't alone because he was engaged to Giff's daughter.

He went on then, the occasional blade of light revealing a brown-faced man whose gray eyes missed nothing of what went on around him.

Logan came finally to Giff Howard's big white house at the end of the street, with many windows all lighted. He looked at the horses at the rack and saw that Jerico and Al had already got there. He tapped on the door a moment later.

The door opened as though she'd waited for him. She stepped out and pulled the door shut behind her and put her arms up to him. He bent to her and was astonished that Kathleen Wisdom came into his thoughts at that moment.

"You're late, Logan," she said, after she'd kissed him and stepped back from him.

"I had to make my rounds," he said.

"Even after shooting one bandit and chasing another?"

He was silent, his troubled thoughts making a dark current in his mind. "I'm sort of hanging back on this business."

There was a hint of irritation in her voice. "It's a good job, Logan. It can lead to other things."

Other things meant something different to Gail from what it meant to him. He sensed that keenly at that moment. "Not thinking about those other things," he murmured, wondering if he should tell her now about his past dim trails. If she was the right kind of woman for him, she'd understand. "Anyway, I just want to get my piece of ground stocked . . ."

"Daddy's planning on your taking over the Circle H some day," she said swiftly. She got his hands in her own. "Supper's waiting."

That was Gail's way.

The three others waited for him, Gifford Howard, Sheriff Jerico Jones, And Deputy Sheriff Al Macklin. It was Howard who dominated the group. He was a man common to the times; the look of a hawk about him, stern, sharp-eyed and the air of self-assurance that comes wth hard-earned wealth. He touched the straw-colored mustache below his curved nose and said, "Gail said you might be late."

They were all waiting for his account of the afternoon's happening and he told them about it while Gail placed the dinner on the table. When Logan finished, Giff Howard, with an emphasis that challenged all present, said, "First attempted holdup since you come to town, Logan."

"That's right," Jerico agreed amiably. "Before that, seems like some ranny was trying it every other week."

Al Macklin kept his eyes lowered and said nothing at all.

"Let's sit up," Gail said commandingly, and they all gathered around the table and Giff Howard mumbled a hasty blessing and they began eating, a serious business that occupied each man's attention and where small talk was frowned on as an unholy breach of etiquette.

Halfway through supper there came a knock on the door and Gail rose, frowning in irritation, and went through the house to answer it. She came back in a moment, looking at Logan.

"It's a man from across the tracks," she said, frowning disapproval. "Somebody's tearing things up over there. I believe he said it was the Candlish brothers."

Logan arose immediately, pushing back his chair and reaching for his hat.

Gail stared at him. "You're not going over there right now?" she asked incredulously.

"They pay taxes, too," Logan said, pausing.

"Want me along?" Jerico asked, glancing sidelong at Giff. Macklin scowled down at his plate and Giff Howard went right on eating.

Logan shook his head and went past Gail, through the house and out the door. He swung down the steps and hurried out to the rack and untied Jerico's horse and mounted and trotted down the street, crossing the railroad tracks, and turned down the dimly lighted street that held Dutch Annie's dance hall. He remembered the expressions on Gail's face and on Howard's, similar expressions of annoyance. It was plain that these two didn't like their plans interfered with—not even by his job.

He could hear the shouts and scuffling inside as he came up the stairs and a chair sailed through the window with a crash of glass and splintering of wood. He pushed the door open and saw Aaron and Faron back to back, slugging it out with two cowhands from the Circle H. Duke was jeering on the sidelines.

Logan was among them before they knew he was there. He swung a long arm around Aaron's neck and yanked him away from Faron and then pulled his gun and wheeled around.

That stopped them deadstill, freezing them, all, that is, except Faron, who went on struggling with a Circle H hand. Logan let Aaron go and reached for Faron and shoved him viciously into the wall.

He got up fighting mad and ran two steps toward Logan before he saw the Colt pointing at his middle. He halted in midstride and stood there stiffly, breathing hard, his nostrils flaring. Aaron moved to his side.

"Can't have no fun around here no more," he said.

The girls were peering through the door, frightened, and one of them was crying.

"Depends on what you call fun," Logan said. "You boys better light out. All of you."

Annie pushed into the room and stood inside the doorway, her hands on her ample hips. "I like a lively crowd," she declared, "but me place has to be orderly. I'll have no rough-housing around me girls, all of which are refined young ladies. Now out with you like the constable says, while you're all together in one whole piece!"

They filed silently through the door. Faron paused outside the door and said, "We'll be back, four of us next time."

Logan holstered his gun. "Quit calling the same old dance, Faron," he said.

Aaron grabbed Faron's arm and said, "Let's go."

They disappeared and Annie surveyed the room with rueful eyes. She was a tall woman, ageless, and her once-great beauty still clung to her in her eyes and complexion. Why she was called Dutch Annie, no one knew; her Irish brogue was as broad as her adequate hips.

"I don't know what started it, Logan," she apologized.

"Don't matter," Logan said. "But I'm getting complaints, Annie. I was at the Howard's when Swampy knocked at the door."

She sniffed. "Go back there, son, and tell them it was a false alarm."

"You know Giff Howard better than that."

Smilingly, she agreed with a quick nod of her head. "Aye, I know him well, son, better than most think. He comes now and again to see one of me girls."

"Where was Jeb when all the ruckus started?" Logan asked.

Annie's green eyes twinkled.

"Don't want to hear about Giff, eh? Well, I don't blame you. That big bear Jeb, I don't know where he is; he's been missing for a long time. But Logan, me boy, listen—things are shaping up. Take care, my young friend."

"Thanks, Annie, I will," Logan said, and went out into the night, not giving any more significance to her warning than a friendly word at parting.

The three Candlish brothers went down the street and Aaron, in the lead, pushed open the batwing doors of the Golden Slipper. He stopped suddenly and said, "Well, damn me!"

Brother Jeb Candlish stood at the bar, hoisting a drink to his bearded face. Even though he caught sight of them in the back bar mirror, he kept on with his drink and didn't turn as they came up beside him.

A black-bearded giant of a man, he told the barkeeper to pour another and then he said, "Just got back."

Aaron sniffed. "You smell it, Jeb."

"What happened whilst I been gone?" Jeb rumbled, his big, dirty hand swallowing the shot glass.

"Not much of anything," Aaron said. Duke and Faron remained silent.

"Hell you say," Jeb said, and drained his second drink. His clothing was stained with grease and dirt and his face behind the mat of whiskers was dirtier than usual. "Seems the constable got another holdup notched on his pistol."

"Well, yes, that," Aaron said. He glanced around the room and edged toward a clear space at the end of the bar. Jeb followed him, staring fixedly at his younger brother. Faron and Duke stood at their back and they formed a little island in the crowd eddying around them.

"Tell him about Red, Aaron," Duke prompted.

Aaron scowled. "Ain't nothing," he said.

Jeb stared at him unsmilingly. "Go on," he ordered.

"This feller, Red something or other, we come up on him down below Red Creek, just after Logan gunned down his buddy," Aaron explained. "We sent him out to the ranch." He wrinkled his nose. "Damn if you don't smell bad, brother Jeb."

"Who cares about smell if we can swing it," Jeb said. "Now, I saw you when you all come in. What you been up to?"

"Ain't that like Jeb?" Aaron complained. "We had a few drinks down at Dutch Annie's. We got into a little scrape, is all, nothing much."

"We got to be careful," Jeb said ominously.

"Wasn't nothing," Aaron said. "In the olden days nobody would of said a word. That fool constable . . ."

"This ain't the olden days," Jeb said, and his hand streaked out and got Aaron's shirt front. "Aaron, you're full of meanness. Can't leave the place a minute without you're stirrin' something up. We got to be careful."

"We should all go out there and wait for Logan," Aaron said sullenly. "Can't let him get away with pushin' us around."

"Leave him be," Jeb said. "Now stay out o' mischief. I got to get on back and my best advice to you three is get back to Snaketrack and stay there until we get everything lined out."

He glared at each of them and stalked away.

They watched him out the door and Duke said, "Well, you heard him."

Aaron snarled, "We're gonna wait for that law before we go back."

CHAPTER FIVE

Supper was over when Logan got back to the Howard house. Giff Howard, Jerico Jones, and Al Macklin still sat at the big round table in the dining room, engaged in desultory conversation, working up to the point of this evening which hadn't gone well at all. Macklin's dark, narrow face still held a discontented scowl.

Logan stood still while Gail tied an apron around his lean hips. He scraped out the plates and stacked them on the kitchen table. He was quick and deft for such a big man and he made as little noise as possible so he could hear what went on in the dining room.

Gail was busy between dining room and kitchen, bringing in the remains of fried chicken and dinner leftovers.

"Daddy and Jerico think you're the one has the best chance against the possible contenders, Logan. I had tea with Kate Johnson yesterday and she told me Jeb Candlish would either have a candidate or run himself."

Her words must have got Howard and Jones on their main subject, for Logan heard them raise their voices out of their idle small talk. He also heard Al Macklin's argumentative undertone.

Logan looked at Gail as she got out the dishpan. She was a tall, queenly girl with a gift for talk. It was hard, he reflected, for a man to know what was in her mind, though, in spite of the talk. But he had an idea what was there for he'd been seeing her since Giff Howard brought him home for his first supper here, nearly a year ago. He wanted to warn her, to tell her she'd better go slow on her ambitions for Logan Marlowe.

"They're putting their money on a dark horse," he said.

She had the dishes in the pan and she poured hot water over them from the black teakettle and slammed it back on the stove good-naturedly. She came back to him, looking up at him, rolling her sleeves up over softly rounded white arms. "I don't think so, Logan. They know what they're doing." There was a hard certainty about her that disturbed him.

"No," he said. "They just think they do." He started to go on and then stopped, looking down at her capable hands resting on the dishpan.

Gail spoke again. He noticed the hard streak of common sense break through her prettiness and he didn't know if he liked it or not. "It isn't like you aren't well known," she said. "Why, in just a year people have got to know you well. And they all like you, everyone in town."

"Guess there's no harm in wishing," he said dryly. If only Giff and Jerico knew how things really were, it wouldn't be so bad. That is, if they really wanted to go on, after learning about his past. He went to the doorway and leaned the point of his shoulder against the frame and listened to the two men arguing quietly about the way to conduct a political campaign. Al Macklin was silent and brooding. They all were apparently oblivious of him and he looked over his shoulder at Gail. She was washing the dishes and laying them in another big pan to drain them and he went over and bent down and kissed her neck and picked up the dish towel and began drying.

Giff Howard tramped into the kitchen, irony written on his rough face. He allowed his irritation to get into his voice when he said, "Got time, Logan?"

"I'll be through here in a bit, Mr. Howard," Logan said.

Gail tried to take the dish towel from him. "You run along," she said. "I'll take care of this."

"No," Logan said, and went on drying the dishes.

Giff Howard snorted and tramped back into the dining room. Secretly, he was pleased. He was tired of men who jumped whenever he spoke. This big, slow-moving Marlowe didn't spook easy. To Gifford Howard, who could sense the shape of things to come, the country needed more men like Logan Marlowe.

"But there ain't many like him," he confided to Jerico, while Al Macklin sat there, jealousy tightening his insides, but caution keeping him silent.

They were through with the dishes too soon. Logan walked into the dining room and the men there fell silent, waiting while he seated himself at the table. Macklin's dark, deep-set eyes touched him briefly. Gail stood at the back of his chair, her hands on his shoulders, leaning over him possessively.

"What's it to be, Logan?" Giff Howard asked. "You know we're right. Jerico says so, too."

Sheriff Jones nodded and tried to smile. "Us old hands don't like it," he said, "but sometime or other we got to step aside."

Logan eased his long frame out of his chair and went to the window that looked down into the main street. He could see the lights of the Golden Slipper over the trees and the lights from the Silver Dollar, across the street, threw another splash of light across the same trees. Charley Wang had a lighted lantern hanging over the door of his steak house. The business people had long since locked up and went home.

"It's an elective job," Logan said. "How do you know I'd win?"

Giff laughed and Jones chuckled. "Wouldn't have asked you, Logan, if I wasn't dead certain you'd win hands down. That Candlish outfit can't corral more than four votes. Not many more, anyway."

"I've been here a year," Logan said. "People don't know me well enough." He wondered why he was putting blocks in the way. He should jump at the chance, he told himself. Being sheriff would be even better than his present job for giving him time to work on the ranch he was planning. He told himself he should go ahead without thinking about it and yet he stood there with his back on the richest cattleman in the country, with all the goodness going out of his day. He heard the floor creak as Giff Howard came over to stand beside him.

"Durn it all, Logan," he said testily. "Don't take a lifetime to get to know a man. We've seen enough of you to know we can't go wrong putting you in office. Jerico's a little man, but them boots of his are almighty big and we figure your feet's the same size."

"I got to have my say," Al blurted.

"You wait, you," Giff said without turning his head.

Listening to them, Logan wondered what they'd think if they really knew the truth. It was only yesterday, he thought, that as Joe Curran he was on the other side of the fence. He got out of the gang and he felt lucky every time he remembered. He'd ridden away from the wild bunch and Haymes was the town he'd liked most in his travels since, and everything fell into place for him to stay.

Maybe he wasn't the first outlaw to become a peace officer and he would not be the last, he thought, but there was a difference. The difference, he told himself, is the fact that it's me, Logan Marlowe. That's what makes it so different from all the others, the peace officers who'd once been on the other side.

"You've made a good town marshal, Logan," Jerico said.

"Constable," Logan corrected.

"I've made a good deputy, haven't I, Jerico?" Macklin asked heatedly.

Jerico nodded, but Giff Howard reddened and said, "Durn it, you wait, Al."

"I was lucky," Logan said. He went back to the table and stood there, feeling Gail's eyes on him. "I'm glad you feel I'm the man you want. I'll do it." It was a hard thing to say without laying all the cards on the table. But he couldn't talk it out. There was Gail, and all the people he'd got to know in this town.

Gail kissed his cheek and Giff and Jerico shook his hand. "Leave everything to us, Logan," Giff said with satisfaction. "We'll run the politicking end."

"I've lived here all my life," Macklin said, getting to his feet. "I've done a good job. And I figure I should have Jerico's job. I want to know why."

Giff spoke slowly as though pronouncing a judgment: "Al, Jerico and me talked it over. We think you're a good enough man in your job. But we need a man who does his own thinking."

"What chance has a man got to think as a deputy?" Macklin blazed. His small, dark eyes rested angrily on Logan.

"You had your chance," Howard said, unperturbed by Macklin's outburst. "Jerico's been away a few times and left you in charge. No, Al, you're a good deputy but we want Logan for sheriff."

"Maybe I ain't been nice to the right people," Macklin said sulkily.

"That's enough, Al," Jerico said gently.

Macklin opened his mouth to make an angry reply and then closed it without speaking. He stared at Logan with open dislike and then dropped his gaze to the table top.

Logan said, "I'm sorry, Al. I didn't try . . ."

"Keep it to yourself," Macklin said thickly.

"All right. If that's how you feel," Logan said quietly.

With the goodnights over, Logan stopped outside the Howard house. He could still feel the warmth of Gail's soft arms as she held him in the dining room after the others left. The odor of her perfume still held in his nostrils. He waited there in the darkness long enough to roll a cigarette and then he walked toward the commercial part of town. He knew Giff and Jerico would start the boom for sheriff next day and he had some thinking to do.

He was all for telling them about his past. It was the thing to do and he realized it. On the other hand, the rough-scrabble country was wild and big and hard to keep the peace in. There was something to be said for remaining silent and letting the course of events take place on their own. Peace officers had been ex-outlaws and badmen and they would be again. He asked himself if it wasn't different now that he'd been off the owlhoot for over a year. The thinking was there, but he knew he'd never talk it out. The talking wasn't in him and never had been.

Three horsemen drifted up out of the night and one of them edged forward and swung down. He had his coat collar turned up, but Logan had no difficulty recognizing Aaron Candlish.

"Howdy, Marshal," he said almost genially.

A wariness took hold of Logan. He looked beyond Aaron to the two men who silently sat their horses. The three of them regarded him with like expressions of hate and the air was charged with the violence of them.

Aaron said, in a gentle caressing voice, "We told you, lawman, we told you . . ." He threw out his arms and wrapped them around Logan, pinning his arms to his side. Duke rode forward with his gun raised and brought it sweeping downward toward Logan's unprotected head.

CHAPTER SIX

Al Macklin gave Jerico Jones a short, gruff good night, and turned his horse down the alley beside the county courthouse. He rode on through the narrow passage and emerged on Railroad Avenue and then doubled back toward Giff Howard's house. He still felt the heat of unspoken words burning inside him, building a knot of resentment and hate.

Damn Giff Howard for an arrogant, hard-nosed ranny, he swore.

That's how it goes, he thought. Work like a Texas mule keeping things going for a broken-down old lawman like Jerico and then be treated like this. He had every right to be put up for sheriff and if it wasn't for that big, dumb ox, Marlowe, he'd have it. Never liked him, Macklin's thoughts ran on, not since the first day I laid eyes on him.

He hauled his horse up short in the shadows and watched, straining his eyes against the darkness. He heard Logan's voice and then the twangy rasp of one of the Candlish twins.

Macklin couldn't make out who was who, a jumble of men and horses in the night. He got off his horse and let the reins drop, his horse trained to anchor. He went forward, keeping to the shadows, walking bent-kneed on his toes.

A grunt, a curse, and a sharp sound in the night brought Macklin up quick, his flesh crawling. It was a sound once heard could never be mistaken—metal falling on flesh, like the sound a pistol makes contacting a human body. He heard a roar of pain and rage and he squatted there, feeling a warm satisfaction. The Candlish brothers were working over Marlowe. It never occurred to him to help a fellow lawman.

Getting just what he deserves, he told himself.

The thin, excitable voice of Duke Candlish rose above the racket. Macklin could now make out the dim, struggling figures, but he couldn't tell one man from another. Except that Marlowe was getting the worst of it—that much he knew for certain. He saw someone break off, and run, and without reasoning he drew his gun and emptied it at the running man, sure that it was Marlowe. The runner broke stride on Macklin's second shot, but he found he couldn't stop his trigger finger; not until the gun was emptied.

A light went on and then burned steadily in Doc Custis' house, next door to the Howard place. Other lights went on up and down the street. Macklin ran back to his horse, holstering his gun.

He got on the horse, feeling excitement and a glow of triumph as he turned back the way he had come.

Once in the stable he unsaddled his horse and turned it in the corral. He went to his room in the Harvey House, across the tracks from the railroad station, on the good side of town.

In his room he dumped the spent shells in a buckskin bag containing other empty shell cases. He cleaned and reloaded his gun. Then he undressed and went to bed.

Lying there in the darkness, he grinned. Guess they won't be running Logan Marlowe, he told himself. Not unless they can run a dead man.

Logan Marlowe felt the wiry strength of Aaron as the man wrapped long arms around him, pinning him for a moment. He was taken by surprise and did not struggle for a moment while Duke urged his horse forward. Logan could see the upraised gun and he tipped his head and gave a powerful surge as the gun came down, clipping Aaron on the shoulder.

Aaron gave a roar of pain, but his anguished sounds choked off when Logan hit him, knocking him back into Duke's horse. Logan reached out and grabbed Duke and pulled him headlong from the saddle, cuffing him about the head as Aaron and Faron closed in on him. Logan shoved Duke sprawling and drew his gun. Duke jumped up and wheeled and ran while Logan scuttled back toward the mounting block in front of Giff Howard's house.

Somewhere off to his left a gun rippled off six fast

shots and then all was quiet. The Candlish brothers melted away and after the sound of fast-running horses died away it was quiet. A light went on in Doc's house and in a short while the doctor stuck his head out the window and yellow light splashed all around him.

"What's the racket?" he yelled irritably.

Crouching and moving quietly, Logan went along the fence and came across the yard and edged along the side of the house.

"It's me, Doc," he said quietly. "Marlowe."

"What's all the shooting about?"

"I don't know about the shooting. The Candlish brothers jumped me."

"Anybody hurt?"

"Don't know yet, Doc. Stay put. I'll let you know if you're needed."

He went across the road, running. From there he surveyed the lighted expanse toward Main Street. He could faintly hear the pianola in town. He stood there while the moon came out. He couldn't see anyone on the road that ran into Main Street. The Candlish brothers were gone.

He called to Doc, "Go on back to bed. Nothing here."

He walked down the road, keeping to one side, with his gun still ready. He paused for a moment over a dark spot in the road. He bent down, touching the spot, feeling the stickiness on his fingers. Blood.

He thoughtfully sheathed his gun and went toward the main part of town. Giff Howard caught up with him at the depot.

"What's the heck's going on out there?" he panted.

"Jumped by the Candlish brothers," Logan said. "Somebody got hurt—or killed. I don't know."

"How's that?" Giff bristled as though it were a personal matter.

"They'd been waiting for me," Logan explained. "Didn't say much, just jumped me. Duke tried to hit me with his pistol while Aaron held me. He hit Aaron, instead."

"Haw!"

"That give me a chance, anyway. I broke loose, but before I could do anything, somebody let go six times with a pistol. Hit someone, too. Blood on the ground."

"Be a good thing for this county them Candlishes wasn't in it," Giff grumbled. He headed back toward his house. "Gotta tell Gail. She's in the house hollerin' that maybe you done got shot up, Logan. Don't know what she's gonna do when you get to be sheriff and go into Snaketrack after them varmints. . . ." His voice trailed off into nothing.

For the first time, some thought other than his own personal stake in Haymes County occurred to Logan. Did Howard and other Haymes people expect him to go in and clean up Snaketrack after he was elected? What pretext would he have for making a drive into Snaketrack? The Candlishes were a rough lot, no doubt of that, but up until now he'd never considered them anything than just that: a rough bunch that had to be to stay alive in that forsaken country. Was there something behind this drive to make him sheriff other than just the facts that he knew?

You'd better find out, he told himself, *before you wake up with a job you don't want.*

He spent the next two hours in his office, going through wanted posters, looking for a likeness to the face of the man he'd shot that hot summer day. He found a reasonable resemblance to him in one aged yellowed poster announcing a $500 reward for Black Jack Peeler, wanted for Bank Robbery and Murder, in Clayton, New Mexico, Arizona Territory. He wrote a letter and prepared it for mailing and left it on his desk to enclose a death certificate when he got one from Doc Custis.

Then he went to Allie Adamson's rooming house on Cheyenne Street, where he lived.

CHAPTER SEVEN

When Bramer Candlish drove a sorry mule and a rickety wagon into Haymes in 1859, all the land had been taken up except the wilderness called Snaketrack lying south and west of Haymes and the Little Snake River. He drove the eighty-odd miles around the canyon and well into the badlands before the sick cow tied to the tailgate died, either from weariness of the long trek from Georgia or the severe beatings administered by young Jeb every time he tried to milk her.

Bram cut the cow loose and in spite of his fears skinned her out and made camp at a little coulee at the head of a spider web of canyons fanning out into the badlands. It was too much trouble to move any farther, so he started the cabin on the spot.

Jeb was nine years old that year; Aaron and Faron were five. Six months after arriving in Snaketrack country, Mamie Lou gave birth to Duke all alone in the rough shack and then quietly died.

All things considered, young Duke should have died then and there. But Bramer and the three boys somehow managed to bring him through until the last-born Candlish began eating solids. Duke was eleven when Bramer died and was well on his way to becoming a spoiled young tough. Being the baby of the family, Duke had received preferential treatment all his life. He had been the apple of old Bramer's eye and the fierce devotion of the former Georgian infected the elder brothers. Jeb took Bramer's place in the house and Duke never had to dirty his hands, nor do a chore he didn't want to do. Jeb saw to that. Aaron and Faron wanted Duke to grow up and be a man and do a man's work, but they both feared Jeb.

So Duke's death was a severe blow to Aaron and Faron.

The twins brought Duke home that night, not knowing he had died in the saddle until they pulled up in front of the rambling log shack that had been added and added to in an unreasoning manner by old Bramer. For as long as Bramer lived he continued to build a room here and there until the old house wandered all around the slope above the coulee where the original camp was made—"out where the ol' cow died," as Bramer always put it.

They laid Duke out in a bunk and then began the dreadful wait until Jeb put in an appearance. He was somewhere out in the badlands and they had no idea when he'd return. They debated whether to bury

Duke or leave him for Jeb to have one last look before they put him in the ground forever.

And in the background was their fear of what Jeb would say. He had given them strict orders to go back to the ranch and they'd disobeyed him. Now, they started guiltily at each sound in the night.

It was broad daylight when Jeb rode in. He took care of his horse and Aaron and Faron waited inside the big room, waited with guilt and fear. When Jeb stamped in they were both sitting by the bunk where Duke lay.

"What's this?" Jeb rumbled.

Aaron and Faron both began talking at once and Jeb said, "Shut up!" in a violent voice and walked across the room and stood looking down at Duke. Then in a voice made terrible by iron restraint, he asked, "Who done it?"

Faron was crying, grotesque tears streaming down his bearded face. Aaron became spokesman. He quickly explained what had happened, trying to make it easy on Faron and himself. Jeb saw through this, but he ignored it and then took over with the laconic suggestion that they get Duke buried before he started smelling up the place.

They buried Duke up on the hill beside Bramer and Mamie Lou and then they all gathered in the big main room, with its accumulation of guns, dirt, saddles and bridles and other junk, all hanging on the walls or suspended from the rafters.

They sat there in silence, Jeb studying the floor and Aaron and Faron studying Jeb.

Finally, Aaron and Faron said in unison: "Let's go down right now, brother Jeb, and get that damn constable."

Jeb spat on the floor. "Nope, can't do that, not now anyway."

They looked at him in amazement. "Not now?" they both cried.

Jeb shook his head sadly. "We made our plans. We got to stick with it—at least 'til we can make more plans to take place o' the one we're throwin' away."

"We can't let him get away with killin' a Candlish," Aaron cried.

"Who said anything about lettin' him get away with it," Jeb growled. "Now don't bother me. I'm tryin' to think and I ain't good at it."

The twins stared. Exponents of direct action they waited impatiently while the big bearded man drooped broodingly in the cowhide chair. "We can't just throw away our money," he said once.

"Me, I don't want no money," Aaron insisted. "I just want to see Logan dead, that's all!"

"You might think you don't," Jeb rumbled. "Because you always had all you needed. You ain't got no money just see how much fun you don't have."

"Maybe Jeb's right, Aaron," Faron said. "Much as I'd like . . ."

All of them faced the door like startled cougars as hoofbeats came to them. The horse stopped and footsteps sounded and a heavy hand fell on the door.

They looked at one another and Jeb said, "Open it, Faron."

Faron moved warily up to the side of the door and asked, "Who's there?"

"Feller you told to come out," a voice answered.

"Open the door, Faron," Jeb repeated.

Faron lifted the latch and swung the door open, staying away from directly in front of it. A slight man stood there, his hat pushed on the back of his head. He had rusty hair and a two-day growth of reddish whiskers covering his face. He looked at them one at a time and then said, good-naturedly, "Well, these two here did tell me to come here if I could find it."

"Where you from?" Jeb demanded.

The slight man nodded toward all four points of the compass, rolling his head around his shoulders. "Piece down the road."

Jeb just stared at him.

The slight man shifted uncomfortably. "Sort of busted my luck. Me and my partner, Black Jack Peeler. Left him in Haymes."

"How'd it happen?"

"Damndest thing. I walk out of the bank and looks like we got it made. I look up and big as life and wearing a lawman's badge is a feller used to ride with the bunch."

"Big feller?"

The small man nodded. "Biggest man you ever did see."

"What'd you call him?"

"Joe Curran was the name I knowed him by," the

small man said. "Dunno what he might be calling himself now."

Jeb swung his black beady eyes on his brothers. "See, what'd I tell you? We got that circular from Ben Wisdom and we can still use it." He stamped across the room and jerked the door wide. "You come on in. Me, I'm Jeb Candlish and these are my brothers, Aaron and Faron."

"Twins, huh?" the small man asked. "Sure look alike. I'm Red Bryson."

The four of them sat around the big table in the kitchen leanto and ate beans and bacon and sourdough biscuits. After they'd eaten, Jeb pushed back and studied Bryson for a long-stretching moment. "You're down on your luck, Red?"

"Sure am," Red Bryson said quickly.

"What you gonna do?" Jeb asked bluntly.

Red Bryson looked at the three unsmiling faces. "Well, I was hopin' you boys could carry me 'til I can make a hit."

"We'll do better than that," Jeb rumbled. "Did that lawman get a good gander at you?"

"I was movin' kind of fast," Bryson said.

"Think he'd know you from Robber's Roost?"

Red Bryson nodded vigorously. "We rode together. He was a quiet kid, but he didn't miss nothing."

"Well. I'll give you some money now," Jeb said. "And a heap more later on. You ain't got much to do except ride into Haymes and meet up with that town constable. Like old friends meeting."

"What do I do then?" Bryson asked, a worried frown creasing his face. "Anyway, how'll I meet him?"

"The constable rides out to the Little Snake every mornin'," Aaron said. "You can catch him at the toll bridge just about any mornin'."

The worried frown remained on Bryson's face. "As I recollect, this Curran wasn't one to tinker with."

"Just be like old friends meetin'," Jeb said with a bland smile. "We'll tell you later we want you to do anything. Right now just keep close to him and see what he's up to all the time." He tossed a twenty-dollar gold coin on the table in front of Bryson. "That ought to hold you a spell."

Bryson picked up the coin and tossed it in the air, caught it, and shoved it in his chap pocket, smiling at Jeb. "Reckon so," he said.

Jeb rose and strode to the door. "Can't do nothin' sittin' here," he said. "Get on your horse, Red."

Bryson walked to the door and jerked it open. A positive odor came through to him and he raised his head and sniffed. "What's that I smell?" he asked.

"Sheep," Jeb said. "Country ain't good for nothin' else."

Bryson took a deep breath. "You only got a big canyon two miles deep and sixty miles long separatin' you from cattle country," he said. "It ain't deep enough, not wide enough, not long enough!"

"That," Jeb said in a flat voice, "is our worry. Go on, redhead."

CHAPTER EIGHT

Logan saddled the claybank right after breakfast and rode through town toward the deep canyon that held a view such as none he'd seen before. It was a good time of day, he thought, when he stopped at the toll bridge. Hy Kelly came out of his sod-chinked shanty overlooking the river and leaned against a porch post.

"Missed you last couple days, Constable," he said, burping comfortably. "Coffee's still hot."

Logan felt the breeze rising from the canyon. It stirred the neckerchief at his throat. He savored it, stepped down from the claybank and dropped the reins. "Had breakfast, Hy. Thanks, anyhow."

Kelly snapped his galluses against his bony shoulders and slouched out to stand beside Logan. "What's this I hear about the bank bein' robbed?"

"News travels fast," Logan said.

"Aaron Candlish stopped off night before last,"

Kelly volunteered. "Said there'd been a holdup. And you was standin' for sheriff."

Logan stared. "He told me he'd ride forty miles to keep from paying toll."

"Well, guess he would," Hy Kelly drawled. "Duke was under the weather and they wanted to get him home."

"You sure?"

"I reckon. Anyway, Faron was holdin' him up."

Logan digested this in silence. Then he picked up his reins. "Guess I'll ride back, Hy."

"Ain't you gonna look around?" Hy asked complainingly. Little traffic passed his bridge and he didn't get a chance to gossip as much as he liked.

"Going back to town," Logan said, and put his foot in a stirrup as a shot blasted out downriver, echoing against the canyon walls. Logan put his foot back on the ground and turned.

Kelly shaded his eyes with his hand, looking off downriver. A rider broke over the edge of the canyon and rode along the rim, toward the toll bridge, coming toward them at a trot.

"Feller rode in last night," Hy explained. "Wanted to know if it was all right to camp out back. I let him."

The rider loped his horse through the sage, skirted a clump of cottonwoods and came on toward the shanty, where he pulled up. He was a medium-sized, quick-moving man with a two days' growth of reddish beard on his face. He threw a bloody rabbit on the ground.

"Some fresh meat, pardner," he said, "an' thanks for lettin' me camp out back."

He glanced at Logan and a wide grin split his whiskery face. "Joe, by golly!" he said, and slid from the horse, turning with outstretched hand.

"You must be mistaken, stranger," Logan said. "My name is Logan Marlowe, Haymes Town Constable."

"Uh, well. You sure look like a man I knew." The small man climbed back on his horse and rode off toward Haymes.

"So long, Hy," Logan said, and stepped to his saddle and rode after Red Bryson.

Over the ridge he found Red Bryson waiting. The little man wrung his hand. "Joe, I've plumb wore out two-three horses since last time I saw you," he declared.

"You haven't been looking for me?"

"Well, no. Not if you're a marshal now." He laughed uproariously. "If that don't beat all. Joe Curran a marshal. Golly!"

Logan was silent. It wouldn't do any good to talk, and anyway, he wasn't a talking man. Red Bryson was one of the Wild Bunch. "I've been town constable about a year now, Red."

"Much crime around here, Joe?" Red grinned.

Logan shook his head. "Not in town. But out in the county it's bad. Sheriff here is an old fellow named Jerico Jones. He wants to quit and everybody wants me to run. And listen, Red, don't call me

Joe Curran. That's a name I used, but my real name is Logan Marlowe."

Red Bryson's shoulders shook with laughter. He wiped his eyes and held first one nostril and then the other, blowing noisily. "Dang me," he said, "wouldn't old Butch and Elmer and the rest bust a gut they knew you was town constable?"

"I'm hoping," Logan said, "they won't find out. They might figure they'd have a soft touch here. And it wouldn't be easy, Red."

The smile faded from Bryson's face. He looked at Logan and then looked away in a shifty manner.

"You wouldn't be thinking anything, would you, Red?"

"Who, me? Shucks, no. You was one of the best, Joe. Butch always said . . ."

"I used to listen with my mouth open when Butch said anything," Logan said. "I wouldn't now, Red."

They came into the fringes of Haymes and walked their horses on into town. At the blacksmith shop, Chet Morley stopped hammering a horseshoe and came to stand in the door of his smithy. Chet waved a grimy, hairy hand and called, "Better let me put a shoe on that claybank, Logan. He looks a mite lame."

"You can have him this evening, Chet," Logan answered. "I'll have Curly bring him over."

"Hear you're standing for sheriff."

"I'll try it."

"Well, you got my vote."

"Thanks, Chet. I'll need all I can get."

They walked their horses on down the street and

turned into the dim coolness of Curly Johnson's Livery. Curly came out of the office, a big tousle-haired and bearded man with an enormous breadth of shoulder. He said amiably, "Hi, Logan. How's the river?"

"Still there."

"When you going to start stocking that piece of ground out there?"

"Takes money," Logan said.

"I got a few head on trade. I'll let 'em go cheap, Logan, to you."

"I'll think on it," Logan said. "Take my horse out to Chet sometime today, will you?"

"That I will," Curly said, giving Bryson a sidelong glance.

"This is an old friend," Logan said. "Curly, meet Red Bryson."

Curly stepped up to Bryson and the two men shook hands. "Any friend of Logan's is welcome in Haymes," he said.

"So I've noticed," Red said. He got off his horse. "Take care of my pony, Curly." He started digging in his chap pocket for the gold piece Jeb had given him.

"Pay when you leave," Curly said. "I'll see he gets the best, Red."

Red Bryson stared. "Thanks," he said. He wheeled and walked rapidly out into sunlight. He was waiting outside when Logan came out.

He said softly, "Man, you're solid in this town. Solid as a hunk of lead."

Logan lifted his hand to his shirt pocket and got out a crumpled sack of tobacco. He carefully fashioned a cigarette and lighted it before he said, "I got a hunch your wheels are going around, Red. I can almost see 'em turning inside your skull. Don't let 'em spin so fast it messes up your good judgment."

"Who, me?" Red asked in a hurt voice. "You're a card, pard. Spooky, that's what. Come on, I'll buy you a drink."

"Never drink in the morning," Logan said. "Try me around six. I have one then, usually."

Red Bryson said, "By golly, you have changed. Well, I'll save mine 'til then, too. Where's a good bed?"

"Come with me. I'll walk you over to Allie's," Logan said. "That's where I stay."

"Want to keep an eye on me?" Red grinned.

"You said it. I didn't."

When they passed the Haymes *Courier,* Kathleen Wisdom came out the door. She was wearing an ink-stained pressman's apron over her dress and there was a smudge of ink on one brown cheek. She had slanting brown eyes that looked straight at you, and glints of red shone in her brown hair like old polished cedar. Worriedly, she asked, "Logan, have you seen Merl?"

Logan stopped and shook his head. "Haven't seen him for a couple of days," he said.

She shook her head in annoyance. "I wish he'd tell me when he's not coming in," she sighed.

"He don't know himself," Logan said. "I'm going

to Allie's now. If he's there, I'll tell him you're needing him."

She nodded her thanks, looking at Red Bryson. Logan introduced them and Kathleen shook his hand and turned back into the newspaper office.

Logan and Red walked on down the street.

"Real good-looker," Red said.

"Sort of."

"She likes you, Logan."

"She likes most everybody," Logan said.

"Not the way she likes you," Red said shrewdly. "I could tell, Joe, how she looked at you." There was a note of envy in his voice.

"Don't call me Joe," Logan said impatiently. "You been out in the sun too long, Red."

They went down the street, Logan's tallness making Bryson seem even smaller than he was. Glenn Hutchins, ever mindful of fresh air, was opening wide the double doors of the red brick bank.

Red Bryson felt a tremor shake him as he remembered the recent scene here in which he played a major part. He waited, his heart thudding, to see if the tall banker would recognize him.

Hutchins viewed them. Tall and bony and dark, his eyes missed nothing. "Picking eyes," everybody said. "That section still out there, Logan?" he called out with a friendly smile.

"Still there, Mr. Hutchins," Logan said. "I might want to talk to you about a loan. Curly Johnson said something about some stock he'd sell reasonable."

Hutchins nodded quickly. "I'll help all I can," he

said. "Glad to do it, Logan." He paused and then added: "Want to talk to you about something else, too. Giff Howard come by early. I'm all in favor of it."

"Thanks." These people didn't make things any easier, he thought. Every time one of them gave him a vote of confidence it twanged his conscience. Logan saw Hutchins' glance resting on Bryson and he made the introduction.

Hutchins stepped down to the street and offered Bryson his hand.

"Pleased to meetcha," Red mumbled. "Just got in from New Mexico. Ain't had a chance to clean up yet."

"How's the range look over that way?" Hutchins asked pleasantly enough, his dark, searching eyes busy.

"Well, it's kinda dry," Bryson said.

"Man here a week or so ago, from Lincoln County, said it looked real good right now."

"Not too bad," Red said. "About time though for a long, dry spell."

Hutchins stepped back into the bank. "See me soon, Logan," he said.

Red drew a long breath of relief as he and Logan walked on.

"Better keep your mouth closed," Logan advised. "These people around here—they're not stupid, Red."

"Well, it was fixing to dry up," Red grumbled. He

looked up suddenly at Logan. "You're doing right well here."

Logan's lips changed a little. "Friendly people hereabouts," he said. "And helpful, too. I've had it pretty good."

The long, low house had been weathered to a silvery gray. It held a *Board and Room* sign on one gnarled post. The Howard span was tied in front.

"Here's where I live," Logan told Bryson, looking at the team of bright bays hitched to a shiny black buggy with red wheels.

As Logan and Bryson mounted the steps, the door opened and Allie Adamson came out wiping her hands on her apron. "Merl's drunk again, Logan. I was just going for you."

"Kind of early, isn't he?" Logan asked.

Allie Adamson was turning into a dried-out wispy string of a woman with all the worries of her boarders heaped on her thin shoulders. "He started last night. He'll never get the paper out this week."

"Where's Gail?"

"Trying to sober him up," she said, and sniffed. "She's got something for him to print. I declare the young women nowadays . . ."

"This is Red Bryson, Allie. Can you put him up?"

"I can put a cot in your room," she said tartly.

"That's all right," Logan said. He turned to Bryson. "Allie'll take care of you, Red. I got a small chore to do." He went on into the house. Red Bryson was at his heels.

Merl Young sat in a kitchen chair in Allie's huge kitchen. His head was on the table. His long black hair was awry, between his two arms. Gail Howard was coaxing him to raise up and drink from the cup she held. There was evident distaste on her smooth white face.

"Looks like he's had one too many," Logan said.

"More than one," she said angrily. "He won't drink this. I can't wake him, Logan." Her voice ended on a petulant note.

"What's in the cup?" he asked.

"Coffee," Gail said. She shook her head resignedly. "He won't budge."

Logan took the cup from her. "Go on," he commanded. "I'll handle this."

Red Bryson grinned. "He needs a little of the hair of the dog that bit him."

"Not this lad," Logan said.

Gail touched Logan's arm. "If you can wake him up send him to the printshop. I've some work for him." She dropped her hand and went toward the door.

Logan wondered idly why she hadn't taken the work to Kathleen Wisdom.

When the door closed behind her, Red Bryson whistled in low key. "Man, what a looker. Bossy little devil, too. Who's she?"

"Gail Howard," Logan said. "We're supposed to get married."

Red whistled again, his eyes shedding their squint. "You've really got it made around here."

Allie bustled into the kitchen. "Don't know what people are going to say about my place, Logan," she said. "Merl's giving it a bad name."

"Show Red where my room is," Logan said. "He wants to wash up and shave, Allie."

She sniffed and said, "Come along."

Red Bryson followed reluctantly.

Logan got a big glass from the cupboard and put hot water in it from the singing teakettle on back of the cook stove. He rummaged in the kitchen cabinet, got dry mustard, salt and epicac and stirred it into the hot water. He carried the glass to Merl who hadn't stirred. Logan set the evil-looking concoction on the table and raised the printer upright. He reached for the glass and slipped the rim of it between Young's teeth and let the liquid drain down his throat.

Merl Young's Adam's apple bobbed violently. He opened his eyes and put both hands on the glass and tried to push it away. Logan held it, forcing him to gulp it down. Merl's eyes grew large and he tried to break away but Logan held him. Finally, Logan took the glass away and Merl got up with his cheeks blown and a wild look in his eyes.

Logan steered him out the back door. He held Young's belt as the unhappy man retched.

Back in the kitchen, Logan poured a cup of steaming black coffee into a big white mug and watched Young tremblingly put it down. When he finished drinking it, Merl said, "Don't know why you bother, Logan."

Logan grinned. "Every man, woman and child in Haymes waits on the *Courier,*" he said. "Can't disappoint 'em, Merl."

"Pour me another cup of coffee, Logan."

Logan brought the pot to the table and filled the cup again. He filled another for himself and put the pot back on the stove.

"You don't know how it is, Logan," Merl said.

"Sure I do," Logan said. "Everybody does."

"No. You're young and full of strength and arrogance, you're full of dreams and ideals and you're gonna change the world. But the world won't change, Logan. You keep jousting with windmills and nothing happens except you get splinters."

"All depends," Logan said. "This country could stand a few windmill fixers."

Merl Young sighed. "You don't understand, Logan. What I meant was no matter how hard one tries to right wrongs, they keep on happening."

"Maybe so," Logan said. "But it'd be a danged sight worse a man didn't try anyway. Kathy wants you—when you're able."

"I'll never be able," Merl said unsteadily. "But I'll go because I'm still willing." He got up on shaky legs and swiped at his mouth with the back of his hand. "I go forth, holding aloft the torch . . ." He weaved toward the door, a lank, wrinkled man with sick black hair and a sick green face.

Logan heard him singing off-key as he went down the street and he shook his head sadly.

Allie Adamson came in sniffing, said, "Don't know

why you bother with him, Logan. He'll drink himself to death."

Logan leaned against the door and grinned at her. "Allie, you like to hear yourself talk."

"A town constable's got more important things to do than take care of drunks."

"Don't know what it is," he said.

She asked suddenly, "Logan, how long you known Red?"

"Long time," he said, his smile fading and leaving his face bleak. Allie had a world of intuition, or whatever it was that women were supposed to have making them so all-fired smart.

"Looks more like Jeb Candlish's breed," she said doubtfully. "What's he been doing since you saw him last?"

Logan forced a chuckle. "Just like any other drifting cowhand," he said. "Here today, gone tomorrow. Always looking over the next hill. Only difference between Red and me is I come up on a place I like."

Irritably, she said, "Get out of here. I got work to do." She marched to the stove and rattled the stove lid. Over her shoulder she said waspishly, "He'll bear watching."

CHAPTER NINE

Logan awoke even before Allie Adamson was about. He dressed quietly and left the house and got his breakfast at Charley Wang's Steak House. Clem Shaker was having breakfast and he nodded to Logan as he came through the door.

"Stock cars comin'," he said. "Reckon another trail herd gonna show up any day now."

"The merchants ought to be glad of that," Logan said.

"Oh, yes. An' Dutch Annie, Mitch and Frank and lots more," Clem said sarcastically. "Wasn't for them cows this town'd dry up and blow away."

"I dunno," Logan said, smiling. "Maybe we could live off each other."

Clem snorted and slid off his stool and stamped out.

Logan was the lone customer after that. He ate his ham and eggs with keen enjoyment. Later, when the sun was just edging over the far mountains, he saddled the claybank and rode out toward the canyon, avoiding Kelly's toll bridge and coming out on a point farther south, still on the land Gifford Howard had allowed him to preempt. He could sit his horse here and visualize the fencing that eventually would go into the house, barn and corrals, all of it vivid in his mind, as real as though he'd seen it somewhere before, in some dim and distant past, as though this was something that had been waiting for him all the years of his life. He could feel a rising sense of excitement and urgency. So much of his time had been wasted, he thought, and then denied it, accepting the fact that everything that had happened to him in his lifetime had occurred for some deep purpose over which he had little or no control.

He lighted and smoked a cigar, amused at his vagrant thoughts, savoring the tobacco flavor as the sun came higher, warming him with the land. His morning of thoughts done, he cut across country, toward the town, where he met a lone horsewoman.

He kept on at a trot until he met the rider, Kathleen Wisdom in a riding skirt, even more tanned than he remembered. He drew rein as she did. He thumbed back his hat, thinking, she gets prettier every time I see her.

"You're out early," he said.

She smiled at him, and her thoughts were that if a man was made for a country, it was this one, this slow-moving, slow-talking man, who seemed to generate an air of competence and dependability even in the small things he did, as now, dismounting and picking up the front foot of the claybank and examining the hoof.

"No earlier than you," she said, and dismounted. They stood together at the heads of their horses and the claybank jealously nipped at the other as Kathleen's horse sniffed inquiringly at Logan.

Together, they watched the huge dust cloud boiling up into the clear air to the south and she looked at him inquiringly.

"Trail herd," he said briefly. "Reason for Haymes, I suppose."

"I can't forget," she said, "that Ben was killed when the last trail herd was here."

He nodded gravely. "Things get a little rough sometimes. Most people don't realize some of those fellows have been on the trail for months. They got to let off steam one way or another."

She smilingly acknowledged it. "Merl has told me some of it. How they drink and fight and shoot their guns. You'd think someone would get hurt."

"It's a wonder they don't," he observed. "More of them, at least. We could slow them down by making them check their guns. They do that in some towns."

"Why not here?"

He moved his big shoulders. "The merchants, the storekeepers, the men who really run the town."

With a slight shock, she realized that she'd assumed that Logan ran the town. Of course he worked for the city government. He merely carried out the rules the town fathers had laid down. Unconsciously, she was smiling at him when she saw the question in his eyes.

She tilted her head, still laughing. "It's a shock for me to know you don't run the town," she said.

He shook his head, removed his hat and ran his fingers through his ragged black hair. She saw the line of deep tan where it ended, and his forehead was white and untouched with wrinkles, whereas around his gray eyes were a mass of tiny lines that whitened when he unsquinted. "I just do as they tell me most of the time," he said. "We could enact a law making it illegal to carry a weapon in the city limits, just as Dodge City and some of the others have. But we're competing with some other rail towns for the herds. The businessmen think we should keep the town as open as possible as an inducement. Be different if we had the railroad all to ourselves."

She shook her head sadly. "Too bad we can't always do what we want to do, instead of what's best for the pocketbook." Then she laughed and erased the seriousness on her face. "You don't think I should close up the newspaper while the trail herders are in town?"

"No," he said, smiling down at her. "I'll keep an eye on the place."

Well, she thought, *that's something. While he's keeping an eye on my place, maybe he won't be thinking of Gail Howard.* She turned and swung up into the saddle and watched him mount and their horses walked toward Haymes while Logan told her about the ranch he'd planned, on the land that was already his. She listened in silence, saddened by the fact that someone other than she would be sharing it. She was silent the rest of the ride and spoke spoke shortly to him as she left to put her horse away. Logan rode on through the town, amidst the growing excitement that always marked the arrival of a trail herd. It seemed almost as if he could feel the thunder of the herd as he dismounted before the bank.

Glenn Hutchins came out with his narrow-brimmed black hat on his gray head.

"You got time, Logan," he said, "we'll ride out and look at Curly Johnson's steers."

"I'll change horses," Logan said. "This one has to work tonight."

"Ride with me," Hutchins invited. "I'm taking my rig. We can talk."

Hutchins waited in his buggy while Logan stabled the claybank. Then, Logan stepped up in the buggy and they whirled out of town.

"You're too much a man of habit, Logan," Glenn said abruptly as they rattled across the bridge on the edge of town. "I can almost set my watch by what you do."

Logan nodded. "I can say the same for you," he said.

"But me, I'm different," Hutchins said quietly. "Different business, at least. What I'm getting at is this—the man with a gun and badge is bound to make enemies. It'd be real easy for someone with a grudge to waylay you. A man who watches can learn in a few days where you'll be at a certain time of day. Need I say more?"

"I keep my eyes open," Logan said.

Hutchins nodded with satisfaction. "As long as you do that," he said, and they drove the rest of the way in silence.

Hutchins drove past Curly's house, on to the corral where he tied his team to the fence.

"Mighty fine bunch of beef, Logan," he said, when they were seated on the top rail of the corral. "You got land and water. Don't see how you can go wrong."

Logan agreed. "All I need's money. Don't know how much. Curly didn't mention price."

"I found out," Glenn said. "The price is right, Logan, and I can put it up for you."

Logan felt uncomfortable, probably because it would make him beholden to Glenn Hutchins. He wondered what Hutchins would say if he knew about his past. He wondered what the banker's reaction would be if he was aware that as Joe Curran he had once rode the owlhoot. Thinking of that reminded him of Red Bryson. He felt a vague uneasiness take him and he tried to fend it off by slipping into the corral and inspecting the beef stock at close range. He went in close, prodding a heifer here and there, liking what he saw, losing himself in enjoyment of cattle which he knew well and the thought came to him that cattle were easier to handle than men.

He came back to Huchins, still sitting on the corral fence. "They're prime, just like Curly said." He was quiet for a moment before he said, "You folks around here have been good to me."

Hutchins cleared his throat. "Why, Logan," he said, looking at his cigar ash thoughtfully, "not 'specially. People just like to see a hard-working, honest and ambitious man get ahead. It makes sense. It's good for us, too."

"May be."

"Kind of selfish in a way," Hutchins went on. "A man like you adds something to the country, Logan. The Candlish crowd and men like them destroy; they don't add nothing. It's hard work and brains that give more and adds to our wealth. So you see, it's smart to help a comin' young man."

"Still, I mean thanks," Logan said. He wanted to tell Hutchins that it hadn't been too long ago that he, Marlowe, had been barking up the wrong tree but that he was right now and this trust wouldn't be misplaced. He was searching for the right words when a red-wheeled buggy rolled in beside Hutchins' rig. Gail Howard waved a gloved hand to them.

"Kirk told me I'd find you out here," she said gaily.

Logan jumped down and walked over and helped her from the buggy.

Hutchins, moving more slowly, got to the ground and walked over. "You get prettier every time I see you," he said.

"How many girls you tell that?" Gail asked, smiling.

"None who'd give it more truth," he said.

"Fiddle-dee-dee," she told him. "I want to take a passenger off your hands."

"You're welcome to him," Hutchins said. "I've got everything out of him I want and now he's all yours."

"Sometimes I wonder," she sighed, looking at Logan. "Shall we go, Logan?"

"Don't you want to see my first herd?" he asked her.

She wrinkled her nose. "Those smelly things? I should say not."

"Sometimes I wonder did Giff really sire you," Hutchins said.

"He's happy," Gail said, not smiling now. "He's getting a son."

Hutchins untied his team and walked around and stepped up to the seat. "Stop by the bank, Logan, and we'll finish our deal." He lifted the reins with one hand and touched his hat with the other and clucked to his team. "Good day, young folks."

Logan and Gail stood there watching the banker drive out toward the wagon road. "I wanted you to help me pick out a dress," she said.

"I've got these beef on my mind."

Her face clouded and she pouted. "Can't it wait?"

"Afraid not," he said. He was silent, trying to gather the words that would best tell her about his feelings, his doubts and his hopes. "Maybe this'll make a lot of difference. I hope not. But anyway, I got to tell you."

"If it'll change anything . . ."

"I said I hoped not," he told her with a roughness she didn't know was in him. "I used to ride with the Wild Bunch."

She stared at him for a long moment, her lips parted.

"I was just a kid and didn't know better. But I did. Soon as I got my bearings, sort of, I pulled out. But I was with 'em for a spell."

She wasn't looking at him now, as she pulled at the ruffles on her dress.

"You heard me, didn't you?" he asked shortly. "I used to be an outlaw, Gail. We robbed trains and banks. We ran off other folks' cows and horses."

"No one knows, Logan," she said slowly, distinctly.

"Man just rode in," he said. "Red Bryson. He was one of the gang."

Her eyes widened. "I remember him. But he won't tell, Logan."

He shook his head, more confused than ever. The least she should do was tell him he had no right to run for sheriff. And the worst, order him from the buggy and drive to Jerico to expose him; but she sat there with a look on her smooth white face that disturbed him. A calculating look. She said softly, "No one but this Bryson knows, Logan. And he'll keep his mouth shut, won't he?"

He tried to repress his shock, but he need not have

bothered. She was lost in her own thoughts. "I don't feel right about running for sheriff."

"What's the difference?" she asked. "You're town constable now."

"I didn't ask for it," he said bluntly. "It was pushed on me."

"After you stood up to those robbers," she said. "You've left the other life behind, Logan. The sensible thing is to let sleeping dogs lie. Forget all of that past and look ahead."

Logan tried to put down his disturbed thoughts, the thoughts that began stirring up the currents of his mind. By the time the red-wheeled buggy reached Haymes, he'd almost convinced himself that Gail was right. He'd accomplish nothing by laying out his past for men to pass judgment on. As much as they liked him, such knowledge couldn't help but change them some. He suddenly knew he did not want to ride over the next hill. He'd passed the last one when he rode into Haymes.

"Let me off at the bank," he said. "I want to see Glenn."

"You just saw him," she said.

"I have to sign the papers," he said patiently.

"Do you have to, right now? Why not forget about it until after the election?"

"Those steers won't wait. Got to grab them while I got the chance. Wait for me?"

"Yes," she said crossly. "I'll wait, Logan."

She pulled the team to a halt in front of the bank and Logan stepped down to the walk. He lifted his hat to Kathleen Wisdom as she swung along the street.

"I haven't thanked you for rounding up Merl," she said.

"Part of my job," Logan said.

Kathleen looked up at Gail and suddenly it seemed she was withdrawn. Casually, she said, "Hello, Miss Howard. Out for a spin?"

Gail frowned. "Logan and I've been out looking at beef. Imagine!"

Kathleen smiled delightedly. "Logan! You're going to stock your place at last?"

He nodded, reddening under her enthusiasm, pleased, too. "Reckon so," he said. "Thanks to Mr. Hutchins—and Curly."

"You deserve it, too," Kathleen said, nodding and walking on down the street.

"That woman," Gail said spitefully, "is going to fall in your arms one of these days."

Logan chuckled. "Not her. She's independent, that gal is."

Gail glared at him, her face tightening. She lifted the reins. "I don't think I'll wait, Logan."

"Thanks for the ride," he said.

Her lips tightened as she spoke to the horses and the buggy moved down the street.

Kirk Hutchins greeted Logan as the lawman tramped into the bank. "Pa isn't back, Logan."

"Mind if I wait?"

"Not at all. Glad to have you," Kirk said, and came

out of his cage, pulling a straight-backed chair out for Logan. He stood there, his hands jammed deep in his pockets, staring out the door. He suddenly swung around to Logan, and talking fast, said, "You've been around, sir. What about the girls over at Dutch Annie's?"

"What about them?" Logan asked.

"Well. Are they really as bad as Pa—as people make them out to be?"

"Depends on what you mean by bad," Logan said cautiously.

"You go over there," Kirk said. "You talk to them and you know them as well as anybody. What do they talk about?"

"Listen, Kirk, I've seen you over there, and I've seen you and Mary looking at each other. It's none of my business, but do you think it's right to go against your father about this?"

"He has always told me what to do," Kirk said.

"That's what fathers are for," Logan said. "Sure wish I'd had one to help out when I needed a little advice. Everybody needs it one time or another."

"But she's good, no matter what she has done," Kirk said in a strained voice. "She's good and sweet. I've been trying to get her to marry me, but she won't. She says it'd never work out."

"Maybe she's smarter than both of us," Logan said gently.

Kirk jerked around, and then hurried back to his cage as Glenn Hutchins came in with his usual businesslike bustle and hung his black hat on the rack on the wall. He nodded to Logan and said, "Come on back. We'll fix it up."

An uneasiness bore down on Logan as he waited for Glenn to complete the papers he had to sign. At last they were ready and he scrawled his signature that made him owner of a small herd of whiteface cattle.

"That's that," Glenn said with satisfaction. "I'll pay Curly and take care of the bill of sale. You owe me a thousand dollars, Logan, but you've got a fine start toward stocking your spread."

"Couldn't have done it without your help," Logan said, thinking that this was part of the good fortune that had come to him when he stopped off in Haymes and hit it lucky. He'd been lucky ever since. "Only thing, makes me nervous to owe money. I'll pay it back quick as I can."

"Don't worry about that," Hutchins advised. "You'd be surprised how many big ranchers started on borrowed money."

"A couple of years ago I could have . . ." Logan stopped suddenly, biting off his words. A couple of years ago a thousand dollars hadn't meant much to him. He had a thousand and then some most of the time. He wondered where it had gone and knew it had been wasted. Card games, whisky, wild times in Fort Worth between jobs. Stolen money never seemed to do anyone any good. His face clouded with his thoughts.

"What's that, Logan?" Hutchins asked.

"Why, a couple of years ago I didn't even dream I'd be getting my own herd," Logan said. He stood up and Hutchins also rose, and offered Logan his hand.

"I think you're going to get along," Glenn said. He looked sidelong at his son and said in a low voice: "Come outside. I want to ask you a favor."

Outside on the street, Glenn looked uncomfortable for a moment and then, like a man going in icy water, took a deep breath, saying, "Can't we do anything about Dutch Annie's saloon, Logan?"

"Just what do you want done, Mr. Hutchins?"

"I don't know." Hutchins shook his head despairingly. "My boy's getting right interested in one of those girls over there, Logan. I don't know what to do."

"He'll probably get over it," Logan said. "Most boys get a crush on an older woman somewhere along the line."

"It's not just an older woman," Hutchins said, thin-lipped. "I want you to run her out of town, Logan."

Logan glanced at him sharply. "I can't do that, Mr. Hutchins."

"Why not?"

"She hasn't done anything to warrant it," Logan said.

"Man, I just gave you a start on the way to getting rich. Cattle market holds up the way it has, and . . ."

"I didn't know there were strings to it," Logan said flatly.

Hutchins stared at him for a long moment, then his thin face relaxed. "Sorry, Logan. Guess I'm just about out of my mind about this." He wheeled and went back into the bank.

Gail Howard drove the team directly to her home and left them standing and went on into the house. Gifford Howard came out of the leanto off the dining room that he used as an office as she peeled off her gloves and tossed them on the table. She unpinned her hat and dropped it on top of the gloves and turned and stared at her father.

"Did you know Logan Marlowe used to ride with the Wild Bunch?" she asked abruptly.

Gifford Howard was in the act of clipping a cigar and he dropped the cigar and the clipper would have fallen, too, if it hadn't been attached to his gold watch chain.

"What's that?" he asked uncomprehendingly, as a man does who awakes in the middle of the night with someone shaking his shoulder.

"Logan told me he used to be an outlaw," Gail said bitingly.

Giff walked to the rocking chair and sat down heavily. He glanced up at Gail. "Why'd he tell you that?"

"He feels guilty." She laughed, a brittle, humorless sound. "He is having doubts about running for sheriff. He wants to make a clean breast of it and then have the people make up their mind about whether he should be sheriff."

"He does that," Howard said tonelessly, "he couldn't be elected dog catcher. What'd you tell him, Gail?"

"I told him to keep his mouth shut," Gail said. "Didn't you ever do anything you were ashamed of? Did you go around spouting off about it? There's not a man alive who hasn't done something he wants to keep in the dark!"

"Yes, girl," Howard said thickly. "You don't have to convince me."

It was more than twenty-four years before; Gail was one year old. He was selling out in Texas and trail-herding to Haymes country. He was forced out by drought. The cows, when leaving Texas, were thirsty and they started the long drive against long odds. There was his trail boss, Hank Clever, and five men. They'd pushed up north and west, watered twice and then hit the long stretch where every water hole was dry, every creek a murky trickle and the cows getting weaker by the hour.

Hank Clever had returned late in the afternoon, after scouting for water and told him about the lay of the land, just ahead. "This little rancher has his water fenced," Hank said, "with a stone fence. Says he ain't got enough but just for himself. Can't let us water there."

Giff looked at his weakened cows and shook his head. "They got to have water," he said.

"That's what I told him," Hank Clever said.

"He all alone?"

"Just him and his woman," Hank answered.

"We got to water them, Hank. Move 'em out. I'll go ahead and see can I make a deal."

He'd got there just at sundown and the man came out to meet him, carrying a rifle in the crook of his arm.

"Hank tells me," Giff said, "that you won't let us water here."

"That's right," the tall, thin man said. He looked at Giff curiously. "You're Mr. Howard?"

Howard nodded.

"My name is Franklin. I'd like to let you water, but I just can't."

Howard saw the face of the woman briefly at a window of the stone house behind the wall.

"Seems like a pretty hard thing," Giff said.

Franklin moved his thin shoulders. "You'd do it different?"

"No," admitted Howard with a small, wry smile. "But I don't reckon you'd feel different from me, either."

Franklin turned so the rifle was pointed directly at Howard. "Better get out there and start turning your herd," he said.

"I've got to have water for my cows," Howard said. "They've smelled your water and living men couldn't stop them."

"They'll stop at my wall," Franklin said evenly.

"Man, looky here," Howard said persuasively,

"they won't use all your water. I got . . ." the rifle swung up and Howard dropped from his saddle and shot without thinking. He walked around his dancing horse and Franklin was lying on the ground and Howard knew he was dead.

The woman screamed and the sound was muffled by the walls of the house. She screamed again as the door came open, the sound piercing Howard's eardrums. She came out the door with the shotgun held waist high and the first shot tore Howard's hat from his head and a few pellets creased his scalp. He automatically shot without willing it, without thinking, and the woman dropped the shotgun and the other barrel blasted at the sky.

Giff dragged the man across the yard and into the cabin and then came back and picked the woman up in his arms and carried her in and laid her beside the man. She was dead, too.

He closed the cabin door and went down and opened the gate. He was sitting his horse outside the gate as the trail herd came stumbling through to surround the pond, drinking greedily. This water would take them on into Haymes country, even if there were no other water to be had.

Hank Clever was all smiles when he rode up. "You made a deal, hey, boss?" he asked happily. "Better talker than me, hey?" He saw Giff Howard's stony face and he saw the rifle near the gate and the shotgun close to the cabin door, and the blood on the ground. His face clouded, but he never said another word about it after that.

Hank Clever had been dead now for ten years. The cowboys who rode with him on that drive had drifted on to other places. But Gifford Howard carried a burden that would not be shucked off. He raised his head and looked at Gail and said, "You're right, Gail. Most men carry the scars of something they've done that they wished had never happened."

"What'll we do about Logan?"

"Just sit tight. Nothing we can do, not now."

"Was I right?" she cried shrilly. "He's crazy to think he can tell and everything be the same."

"Hush up, Gail," Giff answered. "He'll be all right. He won't do nothing foolish, I'm certain."

That evening, while Gail fixed supper, Giff worked in the barn, on the saddle he was making. Slim Reed came to the house and asked for him and Gail sent the Circle H foreman on out to the barn. When she called Giff, both he and Slim Reed answered the call. She swiftly set another plate.

After a silent meal, Gail washed the dishes while Giff and Slim talked in Giff's office, talked in low, conspiratorial tones, but she had no ear for it. She was busy with her own thoughts.

Gail Howard was a spirited woman, with a mind of her own. Furthermore, all her life she'd had everything just exactly as she wanted it. They lived in town because Gail disliked the remote lonesomeness of the ranch. She'd worked on Giff until in self-defense he'd given in to her demands. It had been that way all her life. She didn't think of herself as being a selfish person. It was just that Giff had humored her every whim until she'd become the person she was.

When the dishes were done she went to her room and dressed carefully. When she was ready she didn't go through the house but slipped out the back door. She walked down the street toward town, just when the first stars were brightening. From the loading pens north of town she heard the savage bawl of cattle.

She paused on Rawhide, uncertain for a moment. She'd never been out at night alone before. She saw the light in the window of the *Courier* and she compressed her lips tightly and went on. *If she can do it, so can I,* she thought hatefully. She crossed the street to avoid passing Logan's office and then came to the sheriff's office which was across the alley from the county courthouse. She went in. A lamp was burning smokily and she turned it down and removed the chimney and trimmed the wick. She cleaned the chimney with a piece of newspaper and replaced it. The room was brighter but just as empty as when she came in. She sat in a battered chair with her hands palm up in her lap, waiting. Occasionally someone went by on the wooden walk outside but they couldn't see her where she sat. She waited with impatience running strong all through her.

She heard the sound of a horse in the street, the creak of leather and the jangle of bridle reins as the rider dismounted. After a few seconds of silence while the rider tied up, she heard the thump of boots on the walk and then Al Macklin pushed through the door. In the act of removing his hat he stood there, motion suspended, his hand to his hat, staring at her in surprise. He then dropped his eyes and began to beat the dust from his clothing with his hat.

She rose and stood looking at him. "Good evening, Al," she said.

He hung his hat on the peg beside the door and said, "Hello," and walked to the desk and sat on the edge of it, looking at her with cold black eyes. He rubbed the knuckles of his left hand against his stringy black mustache. "Ain't seen you for quite a spell, Gail."

She tried to read his thoughts while a worried frown creased her smooth white forehead. "You had supper with us not too long ago," she said firmly.

He chuckled. "Yeah. I remember. Now, what do you want in trade?"

She flushed angrily. "Don't be nasty, Al."

"But you want something. I know you, Gail, through and through. You ain't had the time of day for me since Marlowe rode in."

"I'm sorry about that," she said simply.

"I'd lay a bet on it," he said.

"Don't be sarcastic. I didn't come here to get into an argument with you."

"All right, then. What did you come for?"

She stood erect, her head and shoulders back,

facing him. She felt the thud of her heart and suddenly her knees felt weak. She gave no indication of her inner turmoil. "You've seen that short, red-headed herder around town? Red Bryson's his name."

Macklin gave a short, nasty laugh. "Herder? Yeah, I've seen him."

"I want him out of the way, Al," she said in a dead voice.

"Out of the way? You want me to run him out of town? Why don't you get that big buffalo Marlowe to do it?"

"I didn't say I wanted him run out of town," she said in that same dead voice. "And Logan must not know anything about it."

His voice was puzzled. "Then what do you want o' me?"

"I'll give you two hundred dollars to kill Bryson!"

He stood erect as if stung, his black eyes narrowing, looking at her incredulously. "You loco or something?"

She didn't answer, but stood there looking at him, something terrible in her expression, a level detachment that shook him.

He wet his lips with his tongue. "What makes you think I'd do anything like that?"

"I saw you, Al, the other night. I don't think anyone else did. You thought you were shooting at Logan, didn't you?" Her face was deadly in its cold implacableness.

"Don't know what you're talking about."

"Yes you do." She walked to the desk and laid two hundred dollar gold certificates on the desk. "I'll bet Jeb Candlish would like to know who shot Duke. Don't make me tell him." She gave him another level look and walked out into the night.

She walked down the street and she did not avoid the town constable's quarters. She saw the flare of his match and the strong planes of his face and then the red glow as he puffed on his cigar. She came up out of the night and he shifted and then stiffened and she could feel his stare in the darkness.

"Gail! What the devil you doing on Rawhide this time of night?"

She gathered her skirts and sat on the porch and felt the boards give under his weight as he sat down beside her and laid his hat on the porch between them. Symbolical, she thought, and answered softly, "It's a lovely night, Logan."

"Not a night to be walking alone," he said, more quietly now. "The trail herd is here. You know how it is."

"Yes, I know how it is," she said. "That's the simple part of it."

They faced each other in the darkness and she felt the emptiness of it and put out her hand to his shoulder. "What is it, Logan?"

He picked up his hat and put it on, making motions that indicated he had other things to do. "I'll walk you home," he said bluntly.

She didn't move, feeling frustration sweep through her. "You don't have a thing to worry about," she said. She wished that she could tell him that there wasn't a chance he'd ever be discovered, but she couldn't do that. Let him find it out for himself. She felt a twinge of guilt that she should have paid for a man's death, but she put it aside. The two of us, she thought fiercely, are more important than one outlaw named Red Bryson.

He laughed shortly. "Maybe you didn't hear me. I'll walk with you to your gate."

"Just to the gate, Logan? There was a time when you'd walk me to the front door and then stand and talk for an hour." She kept her voice light and without rancor. It was an effort. She wanted to seize him and shake him.

"You know better than that. I got work to do."

"Work," she scoffed. "That's all you think about."

"They pay me for it," he observed, and stood up. She took his hand and pulled him down beside her. "Don't be a silly," she said coaxingly. "Just relax for a minute. It won't kill you."

He sat there in moody silence, wondering what really had brought her out tonight. He hadn't been seeing as much of her as he had before—he felt a slight shock as he allowed his thought to trail on out—Kathleen Wisdom arrived in Haymes. He had a sudden feeling of contriteness and put his hand over her small one and squeezed it.

"There," she laughed, "that's better."

The pianola down the street was playing softly and the night seemed late and quiet. But there was a tension between them and Gail Howard sensed it with a fury she found hard to restrain. He was so bullheaded, she thought viciously. When we're married he'll change. He'll have to change. She rose and said, "You can take me home, Logan."

He had stood up when she rose and he leaned down and kissed her forehead, murmuring something she couldn't understand. They stood there until a couple passed and when they went through the layer of light falling across the board walk, Logan saw that it was Kirk Hutchins and Mary Stefano, the dark-eyed girl from Dutch Annie's place.

He took Gail's arm and they walked together down the street. He felt a troublesome streak hit his stomach and he was morosely silent all the way to Gail's home.

CHAPTER TEN

A small black and white shaggy dog ran out to meet Red Bryson, barked sharply and then slunk away as Jeb Candlish growled a threatening word. From out in the night came the thin bleat of unseen sheep. Red got down from his horse and walked into the circle of light and squatted down.

"Had a hell of a time finding you," he said cheerfully, " 'til I got wind o' them woolies."

Jeb Candlish threw a handful of small sticks on the fire and it blazed up, throwing back the darkness. There was a blackened coffee pot on the edge of the fire. Jeb, Aaron, and Faron stared stolidly at him.

"What's doing in town, Red?" Jeb asked.

"Not much," Red said, and took up a stick and drew two lines in the dirt and then closed off the top and bottom. "He don't do much of anything except ride that damn town."

The Candlish brothers stared owlishly at Bryson and said nothing, waiting for him to go on.

"You got a cup, I'd like a cup of coffee," Red Bryson said.

"Get him a cup, Faron," Jeb rumbled.

Faron rose and stumbled off into the darkness and came back in a moment with a tin cup. He handed it to Red and put on his gloves to handle the coffee pot. He poured a cup of the muddy brew and set the pot back on the fire.

Red sipped the coffee and said, "He did buy some cows from Curly Johnson. They're out in Curly's corral."

"Where'd he get the money?"

"Dunno. He rode out with the banker."

Jeb nodded. "Hutchins put it up for him."

"I dunno," Red said. "This feller has had some money, big money. Maybe he kept it."

"He didn't have nothing when he got to Haymes," Jeb rumbled, "except his gun, hoss and saddle."

"After we made a hit up in Montpelier," Red said musingly, "he was standin' in a saloon one night. This preacher come in askin' for donations to build a church. Logan—name was Joe then—threw every dime he owned in that preacher's hat. More than a thousand dollars." He snapped his fingers. "Just like that. A thousand cartwheels!"

Jeb's stolid, unblinking eyes were on him. "An' that's all you got to tell?"

Red Bryson nodded. He sensed a hostility here that had not been present before. He couldn't put a name to it, but it was there as plain as the sparkling fire in front of him, as evident as the smell that drifted in from the sheep herd.

"Well, there was this talk about you all postin' Snaketrack."

"We got a right to post it," Aaron said grimly. "It's our'n."

"I didn't say it wasn't," Red said mildly. "I was just tellin' you what the talk."

Jeb stood up, stretching. "Well and good, so far. These cows Logan bought is a stroke of luck for us."

Aaron rose, too, and stood there staring truculently across the fire at Jeb. "I been goin' along with you," he said, "because I figured someday we'd get back at that damned law. But you keep pussyfootin' . . ."

Jeb lashed out across the fire and struck Aaron in the face with his open hand. It was as though the smaller man had been hit with a maul. He literally slammed sideways into the ground. He lay there for a minute and then rolled over and sat up, rubbing his face.

"Wasn't no call for that," he said.

"Gettin' sick and tired of your bellyachin', Aaron," Jeb said.

"Hee, hee, hee," Faron chortled.

"Shut up, Faron," Jeb said sternly. "Now get this straight, little brother, an' you, too, Faron. I'm runnin' the show and you do what you're told."

"Reckon I better be ridin' back to town," Red said uneasily.

"Sure, Red," Jeb said agreeably. He spit in the fire and squatted before it, staring up at Red. "Me and you, Red, we're gonna rustle ol' Logan's cows."

"I dunno," Red said slowly. "I'm a little leery . . ."

"Oh, pshaw, won't take long."

"No place to drive 'em," Red said firmly. "You'd have to drive three, four days to get 'em on Snaketrack."

"I ain't gonna drive 'em on Snaketrack," Jeb said. "I'm just gonna drive 'em upriver and shoot 'em and push 'em to hell and gone over the bank."

Red stared at him. "For hell's sake, why?"

"Get on your horse, redhead. Me an' you—we're ridin'."

It was early evening and the town lay hushed among the cottonwoods that fought for existence beside the railroad that was an umbilical cord connecting Haymes with the outside world. There was a feeling in the air, a feeling of restless tension, as before a storm; the storm of three thousand head of cattle moving restlessly on the bed grounds just outside town. The action and motion of three thousand head of cattle in unison made the earth tremble. The pall of dust still lay over the town, dimming the lights. But above, the early stars were distinct and clear. Down by the loading pens, the activity went on endlessly, amid the bawling cows and cursing cowboys. This would go on and on, night and day and day and night until the last beef was loaded and moved east, to feed a meat-hungry nation.

Logan and Kathleen had supper together, at Cornelia's, where the elite of Haymes dined, when they dined out. Cornelia's was as much an institution in Haymes as Delmonico's in Dodge. More so, in fact, because Cornelia had a real French chef, one who was traveling with the private train of a now dead railroad president. Pierre had got into a six-day poker session and allowed the special to move on without him. Pierre was the personality who made Cornelia's, and his everlasting plaint was that no one in the country was sophisticated enough to really enjoy his cooking. He came from the kitchen and paused beside Logan's table.

"It's very good, Pierre," Logan said.

Kathleen nodded. "I've never tasted better. I'd love to have the recipe."

Pierre smiled fondly. They had said the right words. "It's a trade secret, m'selle," he said, and still smiling broadly went proudly back to his kitchen.

"He is really a wonderful cook," Kathleen said.

Logan nodded. "And he is right. Most people who eat here don't know they're getting the finest food in the world. The trail drovers least of all. Pierre hates to see them come."

She nodded agreeably, her brown eyes liquid and shining. "It's all very exciting, Logan, sort of like the quiet before a storm. But I still haven't seen any wild-riding cowboys shooting up the town."

"They're loading out," Logan explained. "When they get most of them loaded the trail boss will ease up and start letting a few men off. Right now, they're slipping in for some of the things they need badly, like a pair of pants, boots or a shirt. They always get a pint of whisky and slip it in their hip pocket before they ride out again. The cook was in today with his chuckwagon and near bought out Odlum's stock of flour and sugar. Chet Morley has more work than he's had since the last herd came up the trail. The trail herds give the old town some bounce."

"That's the longest speech you've ever made," she said, smiling at him. She looked at him with her head tilted, the wide smile lighting up her face. "You like it, don't you?"

"Like it?" He pondered the question and then nodded. "I suppose I do. It breaks up the day pretty well."

She was silent, pensive, her hands folded on the table, and he sat there looking across the table at her, remembering the first time he'd seen her as she stepped out to meet him in the dusty, grimy rail coach, a month before. It seemed a day. Yet in that month a warm relationship he couldn't define had sprung up between them. He was relaxed and at ease with her.

Suddenly she said, "You're a lonely man, Logan. Why?"

"Most men are lonely," he answered. "It shows more on some than others."

"Lonely—and alone. You've been alone much of the time?"

"Out here, there's lots of space. Not many people in it." He told her about the ranch where he had lived. It wasn't a very prosperous ranch, nor a large one. The day began before dawn and ended when it was too dark to get anything else done. There was nothing but backbreaking work and endless days, all of them exactly like the day before. He wanted to see over the next hill, he wanted desperately to get away, and finally he had. He rode away on the bony, stringhalted old pinto that was his only possession and a cap and ball pistol that would have exploded if he'd fired it. He camped that first night in a willow grove by a stream. Then he remembered he didn't bring anything to eat.

"What about your father?" she asked. "Wasn't he worried?"

"No father," he said. "No mother. Don't know how it was I came to be living with Dakota. Way he told it, he found me out in the brush after the Indians attacked a wagon train."

Dakota used him as one of the animals on the place. There was never a word between the two unless it was necessary. Dakota wasn't a mean man, not in the sense that a man can be ornery, knowing about it. His taciturnity and hardness was just his way and he never knew any better.

"Well," she said, her eyes sparkling with interest. "What happened there in the willow grove that first night and you were without food?"

"I made do," he said briefly. "There were some small fish there, little more than minnows. I tried and tried to catch them and couldn't. It was getting dark. I got a big stone and slammed it down on the rock under which the little fish were hiding. One of them came to the top, bottomside up, stunned. I got a few that way and cleaned them and cooked them on a stick without salt or pepper. Next day I rode on and finally met up with a fellow who took me in."

No need to tell her that fellow was Butch Massey, the famous outlaw; that Butch took him to the outlaw hideout and that he followed the outlaw trail for the next few years. Butch taught him all the tricks of the trade, how to scout a bank, plan the getaway trail and stash relays of fresh horses in case of pursuit. Butch taught him all he knew about outlawry and that was considerable. He suddenly wished he could tell this calm-eyed woman how it had been.

He stood up suddenly as sounds of shots came through the walls and wild cowboy yells split the evening quiet.

"Guess they're all loaded out," he announced. "Maybe I better steer you back to the hotel. I'd advise you to stay indoors tonight, Kathy."

"Whatever you say, Logan," she answered.

Logan led the way outside. The streets were boiling with thirsty, excitement-seeking drovers. They walked side by side down the wooden walk and a group of horsemen pounded by. One of the horses blundered up on the duck boards with a thunderous pound.

"Keep your horse in the street," Logan said.

The man hauled back on his reins, raising the cow horse on its haunches. "Who's tellin' me?" he yelled.

The others wheeled and cantered back to encircle Logan. One of them muttered, "It's the big guy. Better come on."

"To hell." The man slipped to the ground. "Ain't nobody tellin' me where to ride. . . ."

Logan saw the man's eyes turn glassy mean and the narrow face twist out of shape. His hands curled around the butt of his pistol. The man backed up a step and Logan jumped ahead and swung the gun. It crashed against the side of the man's head and crumpled him on the duckboards.

"Take him with you," Logan said curtly. "If I see him on the streets again, I'll lock him up."

The drovers all dismounted and gathered around their fallen companion. They muttered darkly as they dragged him away, toward the Longhorn.

Logan looked at Kathleen. "I'm sorry," he said.

She was silent, moving to his side and taking his arm.

"What I did," he said, "I had to do. He'd just had enough to drink to make him reckless. If I hadn't hit him, he'd have tried to pull his gun. Then I would have had to kill him."

She felt the violence fade from him. It was another facet of his character and she was suddenly glad that she had seen it. She knew he was capable of gentleness. That day, out on the prairie when she'd met him while riding, she'd seen his compassion for his horse. There was a vivid strength in him and in a way she was sorry because it made her feel more poignantly than ever his betrothal to Gail Howard.

She said, "I'd be lying if I told you I wasn't shocked. I've never seen a man hit like that before."

"I don't like it," he said simply.

"Please take me on," she said in a small voice.

"Of course." He took her action as a rebuff for his own violence. He was silent on the short walk to the hotel. At the door he paused before turning away. "This is a rough country," he told her. "It's not nice at all, Kathy. But some things have to be done. It happens that my job calls for it at times, calls for what you might consider brutality."

She took both his hands in hers and, looking up at him, said earnestly, "You think I'm reproachful!" She stood on tiptoe and kissed his cheek and went quickly into the hotel.

He walked in the shadowy night toward his little frame office on Rawhide, still feeling the tingling sensation of her lips on his cheek. He felt the touch of her hand still and the odor of her perfume lingered in his nostrils. A feeling of disloyalty to Gail Howard made itself felt, oddly upsetting.

A man waited in his little frame office, a sloe-eyed, dark-skinned man, Herb Kiner, owner of the Longhorn.

"Howdy, Constable. Looks like we're gonna get some action."

Logan nodded. "It's starting. What can I do for you, Herb?"

"Those danged kids and their slingshots. I lost

two back windows again today. Logan, you got to speak to those boys, maybe lay a belt on 'em."

"You know who they are, Herb?"

Kiner shook his head. He'd had trouble with the boys before. "Don't know what this younger generation is coming to. They don't respect property rights like we did when we were kids."

"I'll look around tomorrow, Herb. If I find out who did it I'll sure give them a talking to. But I couldn't lay a hand on them, you know that."

"I catch 'em I'll sure as hell lay a hand on 'em," Kiner said savagely.

Afterward, Logan stood in the door of his office and watched the town come alive. Riders came and went through the dark streets. The light died in the law offices of Kimball and Crane, over the bank. The merchants were closing their stores and in the distance, Logan could hear the whistle of the late-coming train from the east. The sky beyond the mountains held elongated clouds that appeared to support a three-quarter moon. A wind sprang out of the night and he could smell pine and sage on it. He sucked the wind deeply into his lungs, his physical well-being at odds with the chaotic thoughts that nipped at him like a dog at a stallion's heels.

It was full night when he went to the livery. His claybank was not in its stall and he stood there indecisively for a moment and then saddled a hired horse and led the animal out of the big barn and mounted.

He went his usual route to the end of Rawhide,

seeing the light in Kathleen's hotel room and feeling strangely stirred. He turned on Cottonwood and rode across the tracks, turning down past the depot toward the dance hall of Dutch Annie O'Brien.

Annie sat in her rocking chair, on the front porch. She called out to him.

Logan put his horse across the street. He stopped a dozen feet from the porch and did not dismount. A girl passed. It was Mary Stefano, and he briefly thought of Kirk Hutchins.

"Everything all right?" he asked.

She scratched a match and lighted the cigarillo and he could see the mole with its pinch of hair on her chin, the mole that had once been so lovely. She tossed away the match and said, "So you want to be sheriff?"

"I dunno about me," he said. "Some people asked me to run."

"Howard," she said. "And Hutchins. The likes of them ask and it's a command."

"No," he said. "I'm my own man."

"True, darling," she said. "True. And Haymes' good fortune. We'll never get another like you, Logan."

He laughed. "Thanks, Annie."

She stopped rocking and leaned forward and a shower of sparks fell as she shook her cigarillo at him. "You bought stock, Logan?"

He wondered at her source of information. "Yes."

"You'll have none tomorrow," she said softly.

"How's that?"

"I can say no more."

He tried to shrug it off as he tested the doors on Rawhide. By the time he stabled his horse he knew he had to do something about it. He saddled a fresh mount intending to ride out to Curly Jackson's, but the livening town held him. Instead, he rode to his boardinghouse on Cheyenne.

Allie Adamson was darning socks when he entered. She had her spectacles down on the end of her nose. She looked over them at him as he tramped in.

"Hot coffee on the stove," she said.

He stood there, a big man with concern on his brown face. "Where's Red Bryson?"

"Cleaned up and cleared out," she said. "Haven't seen him since morning."

Logan got a cup from the cupboard and helped himself to a cup of coffee. "Wonder where he went."

She nipped the thread with her teeth and laid the sock and her needle and thread on the table. She removed her glasses, rubbed her eyes with both hands and said, "What's the trouble, Logan?"

He shook his head. "I don't know. Not now, at least." He drained the coffee cup and tramped across the room. "I got word that my herd has been rustled," he said. "I don't know if it's true or not."

"My stars," she said. "You think Red done it?"

"I'm not thinking right now. I'd better start real quick, though. I can't go out there; the town is about to catch on fire."

"I been listening," she said. She got up with her

hand on the small of her back. "Don't worry, Logan," she said soothingly. "I reckon I sort of changed my mind about Red Bryson since he got here."

"Maybe I'm changing mine," he said. He didn't think about that answer until he was outside and mounted on the horse. Maybe Red did know something about the missing cows—if they were missing.

If they were missing. Annie had given him a number of tips and she'd never been wrong before.

After passing Logan Marlowe, the girl, Mary Stefano, crossed the tracks and went along Rawhide, keeping close to the buildings. Once she turned into an alley and waited in the darkness until a group of laughing, rough-talking men passed. Then she went on until she came to the livery. She stood there uncertainly for a moment and then turned as a voice spoke out of the darkness. She went into the musty darkness inside the livery, feeling the warmth and odors of horses and leather assailing her nostrils.

"Here, right here," said Kirk Hutchins, and drew her back away from the door. He put his arms around her and pulled her close to him. She could feel the rapid beating of his heart. He covered her face with eager kisses.

"I shouldn't have come," she said.

"But you did—that's the main thing."

"You sure you want to go through with this?" she asked. "Now's the time to back out, before we leave."

"Listen, Mary, I love you. That's all that counts right now."

"Right now, yes. How about later?"

"I'll never change," he said positively.

"You don't know. But let me tell you how it'll be."

"I don't want to hear it. Not if you're trying to talk me out of it."

"Let me tell you, anyway," she said quietly. "You say you love me and I suppose you do. But later on, you'll start thinking. Thinking about what I was and then it'll all be over."

"No," he said. "I'll always think about what you are and not anything else."

She was silent for a long moment and then she moved against him and her fingers caressed his face. He pulled her hungrily against him, feeling her softness. He kissed her soft mouth and then he stepped back and said, "We're wasting time."

"I'm ready," she murmured.

"The team and buggy are waiting. Didn't you bring anything?"

"I brought myself," she said. "That's all I wanted to bring."

"Then come along. We've a lot of road to cover."

"What's in the little black bag, Kirk?"

He laughed shortly. "My wages," he said. "I collected everything I had coming. Everything!"

CHAPTER ELEVEN

Jeb Candlish and Red Bryson rode through the velvet night, toward the Little Snake. Red Bryson, a tough but not a foolhardy man, was still shaken by his near brush with violence. Though an outlaw, Red Bryson was essentially a mild man, usually acting as horse holder or lookout when he went raiding. He'd never pulled a job on his own. These men, the Candlish brothers, didn't react like other men. They were a breed all their own. As far as Red could see, they performed thoughtlessly, like animals. He rode now with big Jeb Candlish only because he could think of no reasonable excuse to get away. Red Bryson wanted no part of rustling Logan Marlowe's beef. He hung back, thinking he'd let Candlish get far enough ahead to allow him to drive his horse off the dim road and into the badlands. He drifted back, hauling slightly on the reins.

Jeb jerked his mount to a halt and twisted in the

saddle, waiting for Bryson. "Ride closer," he ordered, and then spurred his horse into a canter.

As they approached the canyon, Candlish slackened to a walk and motioned Red to do the same. The bridge keeper's cabin on the far side was dark. From behind them a coyote howled lonesomely as the moon broke from behind dark scattered clouds.

Candlish stopped at the bridge and sat his horse looking across the chasm. "Don't want that nosy Kelly knowin' I use his bridge," he said. "Should belong to us, that bridge. Don't know why he hangs on there; nobody to use the thing but us Candlishes."

"How you goin' to keep him from knowing?"

Candlish dismounted and fumbled with his saddlebags. "I got somethin'," he rumbled. He hauled it out of his saddlebags.

Bryson bent down to see better. "What you got there?"

"Rawhide," Candlish said shortly. He said, "Get off that horse."

Bryson dismounted and Candlish lifted a forefoot and bound the rawhide around the hoof, working quickly as though he knew what he was doing. He bound each of the hoofs, cursing softly, when the horse moved impatiently away.

"I'll lead him across and wait for you," Red said in a low voice.

"Them's the only set I got," Candlish said. "Come along." He started out across the bridge. The horse's hoofs made a muffled sound that was lost in the deep canyon below them.

On the far side, Candlish removed the rawhide and led the horse to a clump of cottonwood and tied it. Red stood by his horse, thinking, When he goes back for his horse, I'll slip away.

But Candlish said, "Come on back with me."

They walked across the bridge and Red Bryson knew Candlish wasn't allowing him a chance to slip away. He was trapped.

Jeb fixed his own mount and they walked across the bridge again. Once in the saddle, they walked their horses a safe distance from the sod shanty and Jeb spurred his horse into a hard run.

The two came at last to Curly Jackson's ranch. Curly Jackson spent most of his time in Haymes, at the livery stable, and they worked without fear of interruption. Jeb opened the gate and they both rode in, hazing the herd out. The cattle had been penned so long they made a rush for freedom.

Riding headlong, they turned the herd toward the canyon, taking the most direct route to a sheer drop-off. Swinging his saddle blanket and whooping, Jeb got them running hard. Feeling like a traitor, Red Bryson went through the motions of helping Jeb.

While Jeb and Red Bryson were running Logan's herd to death in the canyon, Glenn Hutchins left the Odd Fellows Hall and walked slowly through the night to his house on Cottonwood Street. He hadn't enjoyed the meeting as he usually did. His mind was too full of worries about his son, Kirk. He knew that Kirk had been seeing Mary Stefano. He was too close to his own past, his unfortunate personal experience with women, to assume that everything would be all right. It seemed only a short time before that he'd met a girl in St. Louis, while he worked in a brokerage house down near the river. He was lonely and the girl, Kirk's mother, had recognized that loneliness. He remembered Lora, Kirk's mother, still with a poignancy that cut deep inside him. She was a little thing, not more than five feet, with big purple eyes and long black hair. She had warned him that their romance couldn't survive, but he wouldn't listen. Kirk was only a year old when the insidious remembrance of Lora's past sprang out to haunt him. He was suspicious of her every movement. His watchful distrust drove Lora away. After she fled, he took the small boy and headed westward. He took with him a large sum of company money, the money he used to start the bank in Haymes. Under another name he'd carved out a new life for himself and his boy. Now it seemed that Kirk was following too closely in his father's footsteps. He had to do something to avert that happenstance.

Hutchins came at last to the house on Cottonwood. He paused there in front for a moment, savoring the tangy smell of sage and pine borne on the night wind. He was loath to enter the house and start what would become a bitter argument. Kirk had lately gotten the habit of talking back.

Glenn Hutchins sauntered around his house and the moonlight fell squarely into the buggy shed and he saw instantly that it was empty. He felt a quickening of his pulse as he walked into the barn and saw that his matched team of fine black geldings were gone, too.

Kirk wouldn't have taken them out without asking, he knew, not unless he meant to leave for good. It came to Glenn instantly that Kirk had left like a thief in the night.

Thief! Why had he thought that? he wondered. He wasted no further thought on the matter, but hurried around the house and turned down the street until he came to Rawhide. He turned into Rawhide, toward the bank, still hurrying even though he had a sharp pain in his side. The town was blazing with lights and all the saloons were going full blast. A drunken cowhand staggered into him and Hutchins pushed him away and went on. The music from the saloons along Rawhide seemed to taunt him. He felt the sweat roll down his sides and he took out his handkerchief and mopped his forehead even though the evening was passably cool. He saw Kathleen Wisdom briefly in her second-story window as he passed the hotel. He angled across the street, searching for the familiar key even before he reached the door.

Hutchins unlocked the door with shaky hands and went inside and lighted the seldom-used lamp. He carried the lamp to the safe and set it on the man-high massive receptacle he'd so proudly ordered so many years before. He moved the combination, not thinking at all, willing himself not to think what he felt must be so, that the bank money would be missing.

He jerked the door open and pulled out the cash box and fiddled around with the key, almost afraid to open it. He turned the key in the lock and even then he did not lift the lid. He stood there, staring at it, telling himself that he was a foolish old man, to go home and go to bed and come morning everything would be as it had been. Kirk was merely out for a ride and would be back. He cursed audibly and threw open the lid to the cash box.

It was empty.

His heart emptied, too, as he looked in the box. A great shame overwhelmed him as he stood there. He put his hand behind the lamp chimney and blew hard, extinguishing the light. In the darkness it seemed easier to bear the knowledge that his son was a thief—"even as you," an inner voice said. He stood there in the dark, clutching the empty cash box. Just at that moment the tall figure of Logan Marlowe passed the bank. For once he didn't rattle the door. An unreasoning rage seized Glenn Hutchins, directed at Marlowe. If the constable had only run Mary Stefano out of town, as he'd been asked to do, this wouldn't have happened. A blind, unreasoning rage ran strong through Glenn Hutchins, making him incapable of coherent thought or action.

He threw the cash box on the floor and then groped for it and replaced it in the safe. He closed the door carefully and then went through the outside door and locked that. He walked across the street to the Longhorn and went into the noisy, odorous, smoke-filled saloon. He ordered a drink of whisky from the startled bartender and then another. Flushed with the unaccustomed alcohol, he walked woodenly out of the saloon and made his way home.

His own son absconding with bank money could have unhappy repercussions, he thought. It just might bring to light unfavorable information about his own background. He had some weighty thinking to do, planning the means to hide Kirk's theft. In the back of his mind, a vague plan was taking shape, aided and abetted by the whisky he'd consumed.

The trail crew seemed, all of them, to be of one mind—to make the night a hell for the local law, Logan Marlowe. That was on his mind after quelling an outburst in the Golden Slipper, only to have another break out in the Longhorn. The small jail, jointly shared by the sheriff's office and the town of Haymes, slowly filled. At a quarter past two in the morning Swampy came running with a call from Dutch Annie for help. He placed a rioting cowboy under arrest and had to fight the man every step of the way to the log jailhouse behind his office on Rawhide; when he came out, a lean-jawed mustached cattleman was waiting in his office.

"Joe Burns, drover," he said sourly. "You got a passel o' my boys locked in your dad-burned jail."

"Just until they sober up," Logan said quietly.

"They got a little fine edge drivin' up the trail," Joe Burns said. "They just want t' work it off. Not harmin' nobody a-tall."

"You got two," Logan said wearily. "Coot and Frisky. They tried to lick everybody in the Golden Slipper. Another one, Fred Dooley, was ventilating a prized painting in the Longhorn. Sim—Big Sim, they call him—was creating a prize disturbance at Dutch Annie's saloon. I don't like to arrest anyone, Mister, and I don't usually unless they downright ask for it. We try to be friendly to the drovers who come up the trail."

"Ain't friendly to lock a man up," Burns said flatly. "You gonna turn 'em loose?"

Logan shook his head. "Maybe you've had a few too many," he said. "I'd advise you to go sleep it off. Your men will be turned out when they're sober."

Joe Burns looked stonily at him and turned his head and spat on the floor. "Talkin' to me just like I was one o' them jughead cow waddies," he said scornfully. "Maybe I'll be back, Mister, with a few o' my men." He hitched at his gunbelt and wheeled and stamped out the door.

Logan sank down in the chair behind his desk and took off his hat. He dropped the hat on the scarred desk and placed his feet beside it and leaned back, searching his pockets. He found a battered cigar and licked the leaves in place and struck a match and lighted it. He was waving the match out when Giff Howard walked in the door.

Logan dropped his feet to the floor in surprise, staring at the cattleman. "Giff," he said. "What brings you out this time of night?"

Giff came in to the desk without pausing. "Slim rode in earlier," he said. "Big war talk goin' on, Logan."

"War talk?" Logan echoed. "I don't savvy, Giff."

"Slim, bein' a good foreman, took it on hisself to take a looksee at Snaketrack," Giff said solemnly. "He heard about it bein' posted and him curious he rode over and you won't believe what he found!"

"What's that?" Logan asked, trying to forget his weariness.

"Sheep, by hell," Giff declared, his mustache bristling. "That Candlish outfit's runnin' sheep!" Virulent anger was in his voice and in the flash of his eyes. "Of all the low-down coyote tricks . . ." He stopped abruptly, leaning down to look in Logan's eyes. "You gotta stop 'em, Logan. It's up to you. Jerico refuses to have anything to do with it, but he will deputize you."

How that must have cost Jerico, Logan thought. He glanced up at Giff Howard's tense face. "It's Candlish territory," he said mildly. "They can run anything they're a mind to."

"Not sheep!" Howard cried bitterly. "Them damn sheep will scatter on cattle range and ruin it! Them woolies spoil a range for cattle!"

"You're getting excited about nothing," Logan said soothingly. "There's a big canyon separating

Snaketrack from cattle country, Giff. You got nothing to worry about, man."

"Them woolies got wings," Giff declared unreasoningly. "You gonna side with us, Logan?"

Logan shook his head. "I can't do it, Giff. It's out of my jurisdiction. And if I accepted a deputy's badge from Jerico, I still couldn't do it."

Giff snatched off his hat and ran his hand through his silvery hair. "Seems to me," he said coldly, "you takin' the wrong side, boy."

"I'm not taking sides," Logan answered. "I couldn't act, Giff, not if I was in Jerico's boots, I couldn't."

"You won't ever be in Jerico's boots," he said bluntly.

Logan got slowly to his feet. "I'm sorry you feel that way, Giff," he said in a quiet voice. "Why don't you go home and sleep it off?" It seemed that only a few minutes ago he was telling that to Joe Burns, the trail boss. He was suddenly sick of cattlemen, trail bosses, the drovers, the town, the whole kit and caboodle.

Giff Howard fairly bristled. "Sleep it off, hell," he said. "I'm not gonna sit by and let sheep in a hundred miles o' my range. These wild-eyed drovers feel the same way, Logan. I been talkin' to Joe Burns and some of the others. I'll round 'em up and them and my boys will take care of the Candlish outfit good and proper."

"I got no sympathy for the Candlish brothers,"

Logan said, "but so far as I know, they're law-abiding citizens. If I was sheriff, I'd have to warn you to stay away from them, but I'm not and it's out of my hands. But if you'll take my friendly advice, you'll forget it."

"Forget it, hell!" Giff said spitefully. "I can't forget it and there's another thing I can't forget, Logan, and that is you turned me down when I wanted your help."

"I'm beholden to you," Logan said. "But you don't need my help."

Giff looked at him unsmilingly. "I know that," he said, "now." He wheeled and went out of the office without answering Logan's mild good night.

The town was quiet after that and Logan took a turn down Rawhide and then went home, too tired to ride out to Curly Johnson's and see if his herd was all right, too tired even to clean up before he dropped across his bed and fell asleep.

CHAPTER TWELVE

The beauty of the day did nothing for Logan. An early sun held no heat, and a slight breeze ruffled the cottonwoods from which a bird poured forth a morning song. Breakfasting in Charley Wang's, Logan discovered that Giff Howard's men had been circulating around town, stirring up the trail crew; this from Clem Shaker, who vowed that a sheep and cattle war was about to erupt.

"Cattle 'n sheep don't mix," he said ominously. "Jerico'll have his hands full."

Logan shook his head. "Snaketrack's like another country," he disagreed. "That country won't support cattle anyway. But I suspect sheep can make out."

"Here, I thought all the time you was a cattleman," Shaker said.

Logan chuckled. "Raised on cattle," he said. "But it's all meat." He didn't want to discuss it and went without his second cup of coffee.

Joe Burns, the trail boss, was waiting at the jail and

demanded the release of his men. "They're all sober," he declared. "Every last one."

"If you'd waited a while, I'd fed 'em," Logan said.

"We take care of our own," Burns said truculently.

Logan silently unlocked the jail and the men, red-eyed and proddy, filed out. He gave them their guns. "I'd like to keep these," he said, "but I haven't the authority. My advice is to keep 'em in leather, boys."

They gave him hard looks, not answering, as they trailed Joe Burns out the door and down the street toward the Longhorn.

Liquid breakfast, Logan thought uneasily, watching them from the doorway. Disquieting, also, were the Circle H horses standing hipshot in front of the saloon.

On his way to the livery Kathleen Wisdom stepped out of the *Courier* office and unsmilingly said, "Could I have a word with you, Logan?"

He moved around so that his shadow fell across her face and relieved the squint. "What's on your mind, Kathy?"

"I dreamed about Ben last night," she said, her face pinching. "I just wanted to ask if you'd found out anything new."

"No, I haven't," he answered. "I'm sorry, Kathy."

She studied him in silence for a moment. Then she burst out, "Is it possible you don't want to find out?"

He shook his head in startled surprise. She was really disturbed and slightly angry. Her emotion added depth to her beauty. "I want to find out what happened to Ben just as bad as you do."

"Those trail drivers could have done it," she said, quieter now. "They're wild as Indians on the war-path. But I don't think they're responsible. I watched last night, from my window. They mostly just yelled and rode their horses wildly up and down the street. When one of them fired off his pistol it was always in the air. I saw that much, Logan."

"They're not always so careful. But then I'm inclined now to believe as you do—that Ben's death was no accident. But I haven't a thing to base it on, except what we call a hunch."

"I've some money," she said. "Would you advise me to hire a private detective? I understand there are some good ones in Kansas City."

"I wouldn't advise it," he said quietly. "The men doing that work are mostly range detectives, after cattle thieves. The trail is too cold." He hesitated, looking down at her. "Are you sure it was only a dream that got you started on this?"

She flushed a darker color and looked away. "You always impress one as being slow," she said, "but I think you do it to cover up."

"Well?" he insisted.

She breathed deeply and then looked directly at him. "There were two men in the room next to mine," she said quietly. "They talked about you, among other things. One of them said you were hiding something, that you couldn't afford to get out of line. But I did dream about Ben, probably because of what was said."

"Who were the men?" he asked.

"I don't know," she said. "I meant to wait up until they left so I could see them. But they talked so long I fell asleep."

"What else did they talk about?"

"About sheep coming into cattle country," she said. "One of the men was trying to get the other to help him run them out. He said sheep would ruin the entire country, that cattle wouldn't eat where sheep had grazed."

"That's so much hogwash," Logan said in disgust. "There's no truth to it."

"Are you hiding something?" she asked suddenly.

He looked at her, nodding. "But it has nothing to do with Ben. I swear that. I hope I can tell you all about it sometime."

She met his gaze unsmiling. "I hope you will," she said, and turned to the newspaper office.

He went on down the street. New trouble piled on the old, from what Kathleen Wisdom had told him. He realized that her faith in him had been shaken and that disturbed him more than he wanted to admit. He stopped in the Haymes House and asked Earl Perkins, the old and lame clerk, who had the room next to Miss Wisdom. Without looking at the register, Earl said, "Giff rented it. He's been havin' a few men up for a drink and a little pow-wow."

"What men, Earl?"

"Joe Burns, the trail boss for one. Some o' Joe's men. Al Macklin went up, too."

Logan nodded and thanked Earl and turned away.

Giff had been busy and promised to become even more so.

At the post office Logan picked up the mail, one letter and three circulars. The streets were still deserted as he carried the mail to his office. He opened the letter. It contained a check for five hundred dollars made out to him, a reward for Black Jack Peeler. There was a note from the Clayton sheriff, who wrote that a man known as Red Bryson had been traveling with Black Jack and warned him that others of the Butch Massey gang might be in his area. He sighed and stuffed the letter and check in his pocket and left the office for the livery stable, thinking about Red Bryson and Black Jack Peeler. It was possible that Red Bryson was the second man in the attempted holdup. But if he was, why had he returned to Haymes? The Clayton sheriff had not mentioned that Red Bryson was specifically wanted, but he knew that he'd ask the little redhead to move on.

Logan's claybank was still missing from its stall. He saddled a hire horse and rode out the dusty road toward Curly Johnson's.

Long before he got there he saw the corral was empty. He rode up to the open gate. The feed racks were filled with hay and the water trough overflowing. He got off his horse and scanned the ground, seeing the prints in the dust, puzzled that the herd should be driven toward the canyon. He walked a hundred yards, leading his horse, and then mounted, following the trail at a walk, seeing the deeper imprints of split hooves as the cattle began running. He felt a deep surge of anger as he neared the rim, seeing where the cattle had tried to turn back, seeing the marks of herders hazing them on, toward inevitable destruction.

Most of the cattle had fallen out of sight. One bright red steer was impaled on a stubby pine that grew on a ledge a hundred feet below. It struggled feebly. Logan got his carbine from the saddle boot and knelt on the rim and put a bullet in its head. It jerked spasmodically and was still. He ejected the spent shell and jammed the saddle gun back into the boot, mounted and headed along the canyon rim.

He could understand someone stealing cattle for material gain but this was beyond his comprehension. Someone had deliberately destroyed the herd with only one end in mind—to hurt him. Who hated him that much?

His first thought was the Candlish clan. He tried to think from the position of what he knew of them and was unable to reconcile the deed to the Candlish brothers' past actions. True, they disliked him for the very fact that he represented law in Haymes and had on occasion opposed their more violent acts while in town. But he didn't believe they had deliberately destroyed his small herd for revenge. Direct action was more their nature, such as the time they'd waylaid him and tried to pistol whip him outside Giff Howard's home in Haymes.

He came at last to Hy Kelly's sod house at the

bridge. Hy came out as Logan rode up and stepped from the saddle.

"Howdy, Constable," Hy said genially. "Long time no see."

"Things have been pretty lively in town," Logan answered. "Did anyone cross the bridge last night, Hy?"

Kelly shook his head and snapped his suspenders. "Nary a soul, Logan. I didn't sleep good and I'd of sure heard 'em if they did. Matter of fact, nobody uses the bridge any more, not since the railroad come through and the old stage route was abandoned."

"You didn't hear anything unusual last night?"

Hy scratched his head. "Well, now, I heard a little shootin', but I thought maybe the wind changed and brought it from town. Come to think of it, it's a right far piece to hear shootin' in Haymes, even when the wind is right."

"Wasn't in town," Logan said grimly. "Down canyon, Hy. Somebody drove my herd over the rim."

"The hell you say!" Hy said indignantly. "You know who done it?"

"I don't know who or why," Logan said, turning away. "But I hope to find out."

"Sure wish I could help," Kelly said, following Logan. "Sure a mean, ornery trick if I ever heard o' one."

Logan didn't reply. He walked over to the bridge, scanning the approach. He found fresh sign and squatted on his heels, looking at the tracks. He found them interesting. One horse, two men. The horse had something on its hoofs. Logan rose, standing to one side, and followed the sign to a clump of cottonwood, while Hy Kelly followed, talking volubly. Logan ignored him as he read sign. The horse had been tied to the cottonwood and two men returned, walking across the bridge. To get the second horse, Logan concluded. They had only one set of mufflers. Two men from Snaketrack. Hy Kelly hadn't heard them because they muffled their horse's hoofs.

He resisted the impulse to ride at once into Snaketrack and confront the Candlish brothers. Anyway, he told himself, whoever had ridden over the bridge hadn't returned to Snaketrack. At least, not across the bridge.

"Find anything, Constable?" Kelly asked.

"Not enough to speak of," Logan answered, and mounted his horse. He nodded to Hy Kelly and rode off toward Haymes.

The sun's heat was bearing down when he got to town. He rode down Rawhide and stopped in front of the bank. The double doors were wide open and he got down from his mount and tied up, looking into the dim interior. He finished tying and then walked into the coolness of the bank.

"Good morning, Logan," Glenn Hutchins said, coming from behind the wire cage. "How're things out toward the canyon?"

"Not so good, Mr. Hutchins," Logan said, endorsing the check he'd received from the Clayton sheriff that morning. He gave it to Hutchins. "I'd like to pay this on my note."

Glenn looked at the check. "Hmmm," he muttered. "Five hundred. That cuts it right down the middle, Logan." He looked up at the tall lawman. "Reward money?"

Logan nodded. "I'd have liked to use it for fence," he said, "but under the circumstances, I guess I'd better pay you."

"What circumstances, Logan?"

"Somebody ran off my herd last night," Logan said. "Hazed 'em over the canyon rim. They're all dead."

"What a horrible thing to do!" Glenn Hutchins gasped. "Who'd do a thing like that?" He wondered if his elation was revealed in his eyes and was careful not to look at Logan.

"Hard to say," Logan said. "By the way, where's Kirk? Haven't seen him around for a spell."

"Kirk went off to Dodge on a business trip," Glenn said, his smile a trifle frozen. "Should be back in a day or so." He stopped speaking and looked at Logan briefly before looking down. "You got any idea who drove off your herd?"

"Not an idea."

"What are your intentions?"

Logan smiled thinly. "None at the moment. I'm having my hands full with this bunch of drovers."

"What's keeping them in town? They usually head out after tying on a good one."

"The merchants aren't unhappy," Logan observed. "I suppose they'd like to get it all."

"Wouldn't take long," Hutchins said contemptuously. "Sometimes I think we're making a big mistake coddling the drovers. I'm going to speak my mind at the next council meeting."

Logan knew Hutchins was talking just to hear himself talk. He smiled as he turned away. When he left the bank he saw Gail sitting in her buggy at the edge of the walk.

She patted the seat beside her with a gloved hand. "Drive with me," she commanded. "I want to talk with you."

He was conscious of his hasty morning toilet that omitted his usual shave as he climbed into the buggy and settled himself beside her. She handed him the reins and leaned back smiling at him.

"Where to?" he asked.

"Oh, anywhere. Drive out the canyon road."

He loosened the reins and the team swung out, necks arched, tails raised, stepping high. He had to keep them reined tight. "Nice team," he said.

"Oh, the devil with the team," she said recklessly. "I want to talk about us, Logan."

"All right. Talk away."

Her hands fluttered in exasperation and she frowned. "Sometimes I think we're more strangers than we were a year ago."

He stopped the hasty protestations that rose to his lips, thinking, wondering what it really was he felt for Gail Howard. Certainly his feelings had changed in the last weeks. "I wouldn't say that," he said uncertainly.

"You're not sure," she accused, "or you'd have answered at once." She sat straight and took his arm in her two hands. "Logan, what is happening to us?"

She wanted to be reassured, to be told that he loved her, but he knew he couldn't do it. "I don't know," he said evasively.

She shook his arm. "Don't say it like that," she cried. "You treat me as though I'm a little girl, patting my head and telling me there are no booger bears, or anything else to be afraid of."

He looked straight ahead. "You are afraid?"

She nodded vigorously. "Yes, I'm afraid, terribly afraid."

"Tell me about it, then. That ought to help."

She dropped her hands from his arm, looking ahead as he did, her brow wrinkled with concentration. She sensed a rigidity in him that had not been in him before. Outwardly, he was the same man who'd attracted her on first sight, but he'd become remote and unreachable. She said, "Maybe I'm afraid of losing you," in a small voice. "Perhaps that's at the bottom of all my fears, Logan. Must I humble myself like this?"

He looked at her. "A girl like you, any man in the country would jump in your loop, Gail, and you know it."

"I don't want any man in the country," she said crossly, compressing her lips. "I want just one."

He chuckled uncomfortably and said, "Well, haven't you got me?"

She switched on the seat so she could look at him. "That embarrasses you, doesn't it?" she challenged, and then went on without giving him a chance to reply: "Men are such fools sometimes, Logan. I'm old enough to know my own mind and I've settled it on you, but Giff is making it very difficult for me, and you're not helping any either."

"Giff came to see me last night," he said.

She nodded. "Beside himself. And then storming home and waking me up to tell me all his troubles. He is completely unreasonable about the Candlish people and their dirty sheep."

"That's what I told him."

"But is it really important? Giff has been having his own way so many years, and the Candlishes are a no-good outfit. Why don't you let Jerico deputize you and then you can run the Candlish tribe out of the country?"

"That'd be a pretty tough job," he observed.

"Not with the Circle H backing you," she said hurriedly. "Giff can give you ten or twelve good men. That ought to be enough."

Did Giff send her? he wondered. Well, no matter whether he did or not, there was only one answer. "I can't do it, Gail."

"Why not?"

"You shouldn't have to ask me that."

"Well, darn it, I am asking," she said. "And I darn well expect an answer, too!"

"I'd do anything legal that Giff wanted me to. This isn't legal."

"Who's to say it's legal or not?" she challenged.

"I for one," Logan answered, keeping his voice even. "It might be all right for some men but not for me."

"Is that all you can say about it?" she asked angrily.

"That should be enough."

"It's the same kind of silliness as you had about your past," she said, her voice slightly shrill. "That worked out all right, didn't it?"

"Not worked out yet," he said quietly, feeling his face burn.

"You mean you're still brooding over that?"

"Not brooding," he answered. "But it's still there and not settled in my mind."

"You gave them your word you'd run," she said spitefully.

He nodded. "I did. I'm still not sure it was the right thing to do."

"My Lord," she said despairingly, and lapsed into silence, swinging around to face forward, her hands clasped in her lap, her eyes downcast at the splash board. After a while she spoke: "Take me home, Logan."

CHAPTER THIRTEEN

It was an imposing sight, the rolling prairie east of Haymes. The grass had burned yellow under the blazing sun, a sun that threw their shadows out before them, long and ungainly. To Kirk Hutchins' civilization-accustomed eyes, it seemed a vast, waving sea of yellow grass, frightening, lonely, deserted yet alive. Nothing moved in all the wide expanse except the ceaseless motion of the grass under the wind.

He turned to Mary beside him. "Must be something over the next rise," he said. "If not, we'll make a dry camp."

Her face was covered with a silk scarf against the sun and wind and dust, but her eyes smiled at him. Dark eyes, shadowed, with long lashes, which he remembered brushing his cheek. She had been quiet and passive since early morning when she'd wakened from a short nap, leaning her head against his shoulder. They had said little on the long ride through the day, stopping only to graze and water the horses at the occasional seeps they found along the way.

They had talked themselves out during the night, during the excitement of running away together. It seemed that after that initial rush of words they had nothing else to say, and since dawn they'd hardly spoken. Kirk found time hanging heavy on his hands and nothing to do but think. At a time, too, when he didn't want to think. There had been no interruptions to the train of thoughts, nothing to break the vast silence except the creaking of the buggy, the squeak of leather and the sound of the horses' hoofs in the dusty road. He tried to keep from thinking about Glenn but invariably his mind swung in a great circle to rest on the image of his father. His father had been firm; Kirk couldn't remember when he hadn't been firm and opinionated, but he was kind, too, and gentle, and except for that unbending spirit and aloofness, things wouldn't have been so bad.

Kirk had no memory whatever of his mother. Because his mentioning that subject always upset Glenn, he refrained from asking after a while. His first knowledge of women was the big-breasted German woman who cared for him. She nursed him, he remembered that. She awakened him early in the morning and gave him his food, cleaned him and placed him in a playpen in the middle of the floor and gave him a sugar tit, a cloth rag that had been soaked in honey. He had to learn to shift for himself early, because Glenn wasn't very adept with children, young or old. He remembered the time when the

German woman went away. He was about nine then and had long outgrown the sugar tit but never lost his taste for sweets. He assumed the household duties at nine, doing the cooking and cleaning. He attended the log school in Haymes until he'd assimilated the highest level of learning and then Glenn had sent him away to school in St. Louis.

In college in St. Louis he was a loner. He didn't make friends easily and his aloofness repelled those who would have become his friends. With graduation, when all the fellows were getting their sheepskin, Kirk stood alone, wondering why Glenn wasn't there. But he wasn't, and Kirk went home to Haymes and into the bank. He was starved for love and Mary offered that love and Kirk was lost.

He thought of these things as the buggy topped a rise and he looked down into a long swale, made purple by the shadows. There were a few willows around a spring and he left the road, driving the team directly into the grove of trees.

There were dim buffalo and antelope trails crisscrossing the area and embers of fires of long-gone campers of the past.

"We may as well camp here," Kirk said. "At least there's water." He jumped to the ground and held his arms up for Mary. She stepped down and her legs gave way and she leaned heavily against him. He patted her back awkwardly, feeling the enormous tenderness and protectiveness she evoked in him. He got a blanket from the buggy and spread it on the ground and told her to stretch out and relax.

She did, watching him as he unhitched the team and unharnessed them. He gave them grain and while they ate he knelt and placed hobbles around their forelegs. Then he rose and dusted his hands and turned to gathering dry chips, not without a distasteful grimace. He quickly made a fire and then took a bucket and went to the spring and filled it and returned. He dipped a tin cup into the murky water and gave it to Mary, squatting before her as she drank, watching the way her smooth throat worked as the water went down.

She removed the cup from her lips and gave it to him, smiling at him. "That was good, Kirk." She made as if to rise. "I'll fix supper."

He put his two hands on her shoulder and pressed her back. "No," he said. "You rest. I'll do it."

"You're spoiling me," she said.

"We'll spoil each other," he smiled, and rose and went about the task of preparing the meal. The fire was hot now and he filled the blackened coffee pot and placed it in the coals. He squatted there, watching the pot fascinatedly. It was the pot he and Glenn took camping when they fished the Little Snake. They would camp in the cool depths of the canyon and fish the roaring rapids and the ripples and the clear pools and walk back to camp to fry the fish in bacon grease and eat and drink coffee and loll in the grass without talking.

Glenn was a talker in the bank and in town. He talked all the time but when he was with Kirk he was silent, seeming to find very little to discuss. Remembering now, Kirk could recall that it was an uncomfortable silence. He felt a lump forming in his throat and he shook his head.

He felt her soft hands on his shoulders and he rose and took her in his arms.

"You're sad," she whispered. "You're unhappy and it's all my fault."

"Nonsense," he declared briskly. "I was just thinking . . ."

"Thinking of your father," she said. "I thought we could do it, but we can't."

"He doesn't give a damn about me," he said angrily. "He's showed that all my life."

"He took care of you," she said gently. "He made a fine man of you, Kirk, or at least he helped. You are fine, my darling, gentle, courteous and . . ."

"I don't want to be gentle," he snapped. "I'm sick and tired of being gentle and courteous and all that it means."

"That's the secret of your charm," she said after a long silence. "You mustn't lose that, Kirk."

He stood there looking at her, at the fine planes of her face softened by the twilight. "What do you want me to do—go back?"

CHAPTER FOURTEEN

Logan Marlowe, standing in his office, heard the two shots shortly after dark. The first one came suddenly, on the trailing edge of a long quiet in town, followed a moment later by another. Inside his office he couldn't tell from which direction the shots came.

He placed his hand behind the lamp chimney and blew, extinguishing the light. He stood there, his hand feeling the warmth of the glass, feeling the soft breeze that came through the open door, stirring the heat of the office.

He went out the door, shoving his hat to the back of his head, listening to the awakening town. When night came on the merchants shut up and went home and the saloons and honkeytonks started their best run of business. He stiffened at the sound down the board walk and turned.

"Logan?" It was Kathleen Wisdom, and there was agitation in her voice and in the way she halted when she saw him standing there.

He walked close to her and in the moonlight could see the strained look on her face. "What is it?"

"Come quickly," she said, breathlessly. "It's Merl and—he's—he's . . ." She stopped speaking and turned away, her shoulders bent and he could see she was crying.

"What happened?" He touched her shoulder, turning her to face him.

"Let's—let's go there. I'll tell you as we walk." She talked as she stumbled along beside him, with his hand on her arm. "Merl sent me out for a bite to eat. We were working late. I went to Charley's back door because I knew the place would be full up front. I intended to get something quick and hurry right back." Her voice died away, and then she said, "He's dead, Logan." She cried again without bothering to hide her face from him.

He let her cry for a moment and then said, "That's all you know?"

She used her handkerchief, wiping her eyes and blowing her nose. "I got a sandwich and went back the way I came. Out Charley's back door and across to the *Courier* back door. I heard loud voices when I was halfway there. I didn't go right in, trying to listen. Then a shot and then another. I went in then and Merl was lying on the floor beside that little red-headed cowboy, Red Bryson. Both of them are dead."

He lengthened his stride and they came to the newspaper office. The light was burning smokily. Logan stood there, looking through the open door, and then he went in, with Kathleen Wisdom close behind him. Logan circled the makeup stone and almost stepped on Merl Young's outstretched hand. Red Bryson was lying across Merl Young's feet.

The printer lay on his side, his face down. One arm was doubled underneath his body and the other outstretched, holding a crumpled piece of paper. Logan knelt beside Young and felt for heartbeats. There were none. He tried to find a pulse on Red Bryson without success.

Logan looked over his shoulder at Kathy. She was staring, wide-eyed, down at him, with her lips parted. He asked, "You recognize the voices you heard?"

She shook her head slowly. "It was familiar, Logan. But I can't place it."

"Keep thinking. It'll come to you."

"Yes," she agreed. "Merl was sort of unreliable. He drank a lot, but he was kind and good and gentle. He wouldn't hurt anyone. Why . . ."

Logan pried open Merl's hand and took out the sheet of paper the man had been holding. He smoothed it out and looked at it.

The paper was an old wanted poster. It named and described four men suspected of holding up and robbing a Santa Fe train. One of the names on the poster was that of Joe Curran.

Joe Curran, Logan thought morosely. *Joe Curran and Logan Marlowe.* "I think I know why Merl was killed," Logan said. "I don't know about Red."

"Why, Logan? Why?"

"Someone wanted to either print this or write a story on it." He gave her the wrinkled paper.

She looked at him, her fine forehead wrinkling, her eyes widening. "It—it looks like you!" She said slowly. "It must be a mistake, Logan."

He shook his head negatively. "Only mistake," he said, "is the one I made. It's me all right."

She walked to the makeup stone and leaned against it. "Logan, Logan, what does it all mean?"

"I was with the Wild Bunch, Kathy. That's a gang of outlaws. I was with them until a little while before I turned up here and—and became respectable."

"I can't believe it," she said.

"I guess you hate me," he said.

"Oh, Logan." She came to his side and touched his hand. "You quit, Logan. You did it of your own free will. That makes a big difference."

"I wish I could believe it," he told her.

She said, "I think I know how you feel. You probably think about it quite a bit. Too much. I know this: I trust you more than anyone I've ever known."

He felt he could breathe easier in that moment. It seemed as though a great weight had lifted from his shoulders.

She went on, "Anyway, the *Courier* could run this story and it'd make no difference, Logan. No one in this country is against you."

He gave her a rueful smile. "The Candlish brothers would like . . ."

"Candlish! That's who I heard! Jeb Candlish."

His lean brown jaw tightened. "You're sure, Kathy?"

"I'm positive, Logan. It wasn't a too familiar voice, but I'd heard it before and couldn't identify it . . ."

The floor creaked then and both of them looked around. Logan saw Al Macklin and then the gun Macklin held in his hand. The gun was aimed unwaveringly at Logan's belt buckle.

"Real slick, buddy," Macklin said. "That is, it woulda been if you'd got away with it—Joe Curran!"

"Got away with what?" Logan asked, not because he wanted to know, for it came to him at once what was in Macklin's mind and the whole thing unraveled in his thoughts.

"Killing Young to keep him from printin' about you bein' an outlaw. Killing Bryson to shut him up. You was in Massey's gang with him and you damn well know it."

"How'd you know all that, Al?" Logan asked, his voice soft. "Where'd you get it all, Al?"

"Never mind." Macklin raised the hammer on his gun. "I've seen you handle a gun, Constable. Don't make a sudden move or I'll gutshoot you. I won't give you a chance."

Logan laughed, a crazy, reckless laugh, and Macklin backed up a step.

"No, Logan, no," Kathleen Wisdom whispered.

Her whispered warning forced him to relax. "What're you going to do, Macklin?"

"Guess a lot o' good people around here gonna be good and surprised." He grinned. "Especially Jerico and Howard. What'm I gonna do? Throw you in jail, Curran or Marlowe, or whatever your name is. Throw you in jail and lose the key. You belong in jail, owlhoot."

"All right," Logan said. "Get it over with."

"Turn around," Macklin said. "Turn around slow."

Cursing under his breath, Logan did as Macklin ordered.

"Git over there, gal," Macklin ordered. "Don't get between him and me. Lift his gun out and throw it down."

"Get it yourself," Kathleen Wisdom said.

Macklin cursed. "I'm the law," he said, "an' you're goin' against me. I won't forget it."

Logan heard the squeak of Macklin's boots as the man came forward. When the sound stopped, he flung himself to one side, chopping at Macklin's biceps.

CHAPTER FIFTEEN

Macklin's gun exploded and Logan felt the burn of it on his hand. He chopped again and then swung a swift, savage right that smashed into Macklin's face. The gun clattered to the floor and Macklin flung himself on Logan, gustily breathing blood into Logan's face.

They gripped and stumbled over Young's body, parted and then came together again, in the clear. Macklin threw his arms around Logan and stamped on Logan's instep and fastened his teeth in the lawman's shoulder.

Logan, unable to work free, jabbed at the deputy's midsection, feeling the teeth working on his shoulder in animal-like savagery. The deputy hung on, biting, while Logan tried to shake him loose. With a tremendous surge, Logan shook him off and slammed a short but wicked right into the bloody face. Macklin squealed and turned and grabbed a hammer from the makeup stone. Kathleen cried out as Macklin wheeled and the hammer whistled through the air. Logan dodged the hammer and as it swished past he lunged in and grabbed Macklin's arm. Logan turned, twisting, and Macklin howled and dropped the hammer. Logan released the arm and hit Macklin another savage blow that rocketed Macklin back into the wall. He rebounded away from the wall and into Logan's rocky fist, a blow that flung him into the wall. He hung there for a moment, glassy-eyed, and then slid down the wall to the floor.

Logan got Macklin's gun and thrust it into his belt. His breath came in hoarse rattles as he said, "Got to get out of here quick."

"Don't—don't run, Logan," Kathy said.

He shook his head angrily. "I'm not running. I'm going after Candlish. Even if I have to go into Snake-track."

"I'll go," she said wildly. "I'll go with you."

"You can't do that," he said stolidly.

"What'll I do then?" she cried. "Macklin and Candlish must be in this together. I'm your witness that you didn't kill Merl. Do you want them to kill me, too?"

He swung about impatiently. "There's something to what you say, but to ride with me, that's crazy. You're not even dressed for riding."

The noise of the revelry sounded clear and mocking. "I don't care," she said. "I'll go as I am."

He looked at her dress, a gray thing with black piping on the edges of the little coat that hugged her body. "All right, then." He was brusque because he didn't want her to go; yet there was something to her fear. "You wait here. I'll get horses. Got to be gone when Macklin wakes up."

She looked at the three men on the floor. She shivered. "I'll go with you now," she said.

"All right, then." Irritation brought a rough quality to him. He saw the look in her eyes and he made his apology in his own way. "I've got to hurry. We might get to the bridge before Candlish." He hesitated. "Maybe you could stay with Gail Howard."

She laughed shortly. "I'd be about as welcome there as a rattlesnake."

He said no more and they went together to the livery. His claybank wasn't in the stall and he hadn't expected to find it there. He picked out two good horses and saddled them quickly.

He was ready, finally, and he let her step on his hand and boosted her up. She had trouble with her skirt and he saw a flash of petticoat and white gleam of her leg as she gathered her skirt in, wrapping it around her leg and tucking it in between her calf and the saddle leather.

He caught up his reins and stepped into the saddle. "I'll have to stop by the Howards'. Giff can tell Jerico about Merl and Red."

They went by back streets to Giff Howard's big white house. "Wait here," he told her.

She said in a soft voice that irritated him, "Take your time."

He went up to the house with long strides and hammered on the door.

After a time, the door opened. Gail stared in surprise. "Logan, what's wrong?"

"Merl Young and Red Bryson," he said tersely. "They've been shot. I'm going after Candlish."

That fool Macklin, she thought angrily, *That utter, stupid fool.* "Candlish?" she asked in real amazement. "He did it?"

Logan nodded. "I think so. Kathleen Wisdom recognized his voice. She didn't actually see the killing."

"Kathleen Wisdom." Her head was down, her smooth white forehead wrinkled. "But, Logan, if you leave town after Candlish—that's Jerico's job. You've said so yourself."

He shook his head impatiently. "Merl was my friend and I don't know where to find Jerico on short notice. Anyway, I might be able to head him off at the bridge.

She shook his arm lightly. "There are four of them," she said. "They might kill you. All for nothing, too."

"For nothing?" he asked, puzzled at her way of thinking.

"Don't you see?" She shook his arm in exasperation. "Merl Young is—was a drunkard. His loss is nothing to Haymes—and it shouldn't be to you . . ." She stopped talking abruptly, seeing the look on his face and in his eyes.

"Merl got killed because of me," he said soberly. "Candlish was trying to force him to expose me. Merl wouldn't do it."

She dropped her hand from his arm, her face looking sharp in its frown. "Don't be childish," she said. "You're building this in your mind. You feel guilty and you've got to stop it."

"Tell Giff, will you?"

"He's at Glenn Hutchins'," she said.

"If you think it's important enough, go on over and tell him now," Logan said. "Otherwise, when he comes back."

She was looking past him into the darkness. "Who's with you?"

"Kathleen."

"Kathleen Wisdom? And you're going after Candlish?"

"She's a witness," he said, "of sorts. If he found out, he might try to kill her, too."

"Bosh," she said, with the hardness he'd noticed before. "Pure nonsense. Take her home, if you can call a hotel home, and go home yourself. You're making a big . . ."

"Good night," he said curtly, and turned away.

"Logan! Do you know what you're doing?"

He didn't answer that, but kept on going. When he got to his horse she had closed the door.

"She'll get over it," Kathleen Wisdom said.

Logan didn't answer her, either. He got on his horse and sat there for a moment and then said heavily, "Maybe I'd better leave you here. You'd be all right in Giff's house."

"Right now, I'd say no," she answered him.

There was no answer to that and he made none.

CHAPTER SIXTEEN

They rode through the night and the warmth was gone from the land. The quarter-moon had disappeared behind high clouds, emitting a soft glow, and through rents the stars seemed large and bright and sparkling. She pulled up once and sat there and he stopped his horse and reined it back beside her.

In a small voice, she said, "I don't know whether it was Jeb Candlish or not that I heard."

"I don't get it," he said.

"Actually, I've never seen or heard Jeb that I know about. That voice I heard was the same as the man on the train. The one that tried to take me off the train."

"What made you say it was Jeb?"

"I don't know, really. They do all sound alike. And I heard the twins the same day I arrived in Haymes. They got rather nasty and I thought there would be trouble."

He sat in silence and then he raised his head. "We'll go on," he said.

"But, Logan," she protested, "this changes everything, doesn't it?"

"Does it?" he asked grimly, and urged his horse on.

There were men at the bridge. They made enough noise to pull Logan off the road and into the cottonwoods. He stood in his stirrups, listening, straining to hear, but only a jumble of voices reached him.

"Maybe Macklin is waiting out there," Kathleen whispered.

He was thinking the same thing. He got down and gave his reins to Kathleen, their hands brushing in the exchange. "Stay here," he commanded, "and keep quiet."

"Be careful," she murmured.

He was still feeling that touch of her hand when he came out behind Hy Kelly's sod shanty. The back window was lighted and Logan edged up to it. He took off his hat and peered over the edge of the window. Al Macklin sat at a table facing him, nursing a mug of coffee. His face was marked with dark purple bruises and his free hand caressed a lump on his lean, dark jaw.

"Can't see for the life o' me why Logan would do a thing like that," Hy said. He stood with his back to the stove, his hands crossed, warming them.

Macklin uttered a short laugh. "Just goes to show. You never know a man right off."

"But it don't figger, Al. He's as well put-up a man as I know."

"That don't keep a man honest," Macklin said.

Mrs. Kelly, a heavy woman who waddled when she walked, spoke up, and her voice was shrill. "Knew they was somethin' wrong with that man. The way he rode out here and stared into that canyon. Just expectin' somebody, that's what!"

"Showed up, too, didn't he?" Macklin's gloating voice floated out to Logan.

"Well, I was there that day," Kelly said reluctantly. "Logan denied knowin' him. And that poker face o' his'n . . ."

"Just playing it that way," he said conclusively, and stood up. "Way I figure, they got the loot from the bank and then Logan went by to make sure Young didn't talk. Then he decided that he'd take all the money and gunned his pardner down, too."

"Can't believe it," Hy Kelly said, still shaking his head.

"That's the trouble with you," Mrs. Kelly said in her shrill voice that seemed incongruous in one so huge. "Never see anything right. Good men like Glenn Hutchins, you think they're sharp and crooked. And men like Logan Marlowe . . ." She threw up her hands and banged a skillet on the stove.

"They planned it good all right," Macklin said. He looked at Mrs. Kelly. "I'm sendin' the boys in one at a time, Miz Kelly. Feed 'em plenty. Ain't no tellin' when we eat again."

Mrs. Kelly nodded. "We got a fresh chunk of

venison. I'll fry that and some eggs should fill 'em up."

Kelly was standing there staring at Macklin. "He might of gone across, but I don't think so. I got so's I can hear a coyote walkin' down that road."

Logan's hands were sweaty as he squatted there in the shadow of the cabin. He'd heard just enough to know he had to learn more. He catfooted back through the sage to the cottonwoods.

Kathleen uttered a startled cry when he loomed up in the darkness.

He put his hand over her mouth. Her face was soft and warm and he could feel the outline of her jaw. He couldn't help himself then. He pulled her against him and she was soft and warm just as her face had been. She put her arms under his arms and over his shoulders and raised herself to his kiss. She pulled away first.

"You—you scared me," she whispered.

His heart was pounding and not from anything but this woman close to him. He bent his head and said, "Sometimes . . ."

"Yes, Logan."

He was silent for a long moment and then he said, "Something funny out there, Kathy. Macklin's there with a posse."

She was disappointed, but she didn't show it. "He couldn't have talked Jerico into believing you killed Merl."

He shook his head. "Something besides Merl's death. I got to find out somehow."

"What can I do?"

"I dunno. Wait, I reckon. I think I know how to do it." He stood there with his head down, thinking his own moody thoughts. He could feel a trap closing in on him and the only question was the extent of it. He wondered where Jerico Jones was at this moment and wished heartily that he was heading up the posse. But then, Jerico was in a trap of sorts, himself. He was a man who inspired confidence, a man people liked heartily, but he was, after all, a man, a human being and subject to pressures like anyone else.

Logan heaved a sigh. It was all in his hands. Whatever happened, he had to face up to it alone, just as he'd ridden alone all the days of his life.

Kathy sensed the hesitation in him and knew it wasn't fear. She was attracted to him, more so than to any man she'd previously met. She knew him well, for in the brief time they'd had together she'd formed her opinion and in the past she'd found her judgment sound. She said, "Logan, where did Macklin get the men for his posse?"

"Mostly men in the saloon. Probably a few of the drovers looking for excitement. What does it matter?"

"If they came from the saloon," she said, "maybe the drink is wearing off."

He nodded. She was smart. "Macklin's sending them in one at a time to eat," he said. "I'll corral one of them and see what I can find out."

Her hand rested on his arm. "It's dangerous," she said. "Please be careful, Logan."

"You'll be all right here," he said.

"I'm not worried about myself," she said softly.

He went out into the darkness, toward the shanty. He wasn't quite there when he heard the pound of more horsemen pouring down the road from the direction of Haymes.

He drifted back from the shanty and circled widely and came up through the clump of cottonwoods on the far side. He was barely out of sight when the group of horsemen pulled up at the bridge. He heard the loud and querulous voice of Giff Howard.

"Where's Macklin?" he demanded.

Macklin had come from the shanty and now he moved out of the shadows and said, "Here I am, Mr. Howard."

With the arrival of Giff Howard, Logan began moving out of concealment, but Giff Howard's next words stopped him.

"You'll never get Marlowe here," he said roughly. "Anyway, he's not what I'm after. You know there's sheep across that canyon and I won't rest 'til every damn one of them is dead or scattered."

"Why, Mr. Howard, that's against the law," Macklin said smoothly, "destroying people's property that way." His voice held a note of mockery.

"To hell with that!" Giff roared. "You say you want to be sheriff. Well, you can be. All we got to do is cross that bridge and kill sheep and Candlishes and you got it made! You got my word."

"Mr. Howard, I'm not after sheep nor Candlish people. I'm looking for Logan Marlowe. And if you'll take my advice, you'll leave Candlish alone. There might be just a little more over there than you can handle."

Slim Reed, Howard's foreman, spoke up in a soft menacing voice. "Boss, we're wastin' time. Let's move on over. There ain't a sheepman livin' can stop us."

"Listen, Slim. Maybe you didn't get it, and you too, Mr. Howard. Your boy Marlowe killed two men tonight and held up the bank. You help us get him and later on we'll help you with your Candlish troubles. How's that?"

Howard dismounted heavily and stood there beside his horse, tightening a cinch. He looked up at Slim Reed and said, "What about it, Slim?"

"Whatever you say, boss," Slim answered, and slid to the ground. The rest of the horsemen dismounted and the group moved toward the bridge, merging with the others.

Logan shook his head in puzzlement. Al Macklin wanted to be sheriff very badly and yet he hadn't traded with Giff Howard. Giff was powerful enough to make good on his promise, too. Yet Al Macklin for some reason had opposed him. Suddenly, Logan nodded, remembering what Kathleen had said about Macklin and Candlish being in cahoots. It surely seemed that way now, more than ever.

He moved through the darkness, again circling and coming up behind the shanty. He sensed rather than saw the motion and threw himself on the ground as a gun went off. He scurried along the ground as guns went off in front of the shanty. A man yelled, "Stay at the bridge, a couple o' you!"

An exultant voice shouted, "I think I hit him!"

Logan half rose and went through the sage at a crouch as guns blasted the night and he heard the angry drone of lead. He straightened and began running. A figure rose up out of the sage and Logan swept his gun through the air. It never landed. Something exploded against his head. He tried to put his gun up, but the ground seemed to bounce up and knock it out of his hand. He went down heavily. He faintly heard someone shout, "I got him!" His fingers grabbed for the gun and again something exploded on top of his head.

CHAPTER SEVENTEEN

Logan didn't lose consciousness. Rough hand grabbed him and hauled him to his feet. Someon ran through the sage with a lantern and in a few min utes Logan was in a circle of grim faces, drovers Circle H men, plus a few hangers-on from the Long horn and Golden Slipper. And then he saw Glenr Hutchins with the wrathful look of an angry lion or his bleak face.

Glenn fastened his burning eyes on Logan "Why'd you do it?" he muttered. "Why? Wasn't I square with you?"

"I don't think you'd believe me," Logan said, "nc matter what I tell you."

Macklin's fist smashed into his face. "Shut up!" roared the deputy.

A rope whistled ominously through the air a someone whirled it around and around. "Let's us this! Them cottonwoods over there are might handy."

"That's the money!" another shouted.

Hutchins alone protested. "I guess I ought to go along, but I can't. He's going back and having a trial."

"I think it's a waste of time!"

A thunder of hoofbeats welled up in the night, and all of them turned, startled. The horses were among them, scattering them like straws in the wind, snorting, squealing, maddened horses. The men were knocked aside, and momentarily Logan stood alone. He grabbed the horn of the saddle and jabbed the horse viciously in the flank. They were out like that, and with a bound Logan landed in the saddle, and they were pounding through the night with guns going off behind them and the lead making angry sounds. A rash of outraged shouts broke out.

Out away from the posse, still pounding along, he leaned over and put his hand on Kathleen's shoulder. "I wish I'd met you ten years ago."

"Do you, Logan?" she asked steadily. "It'd be tiresome by now."

"Maybe," he said.

They rode in silence for a time. "You're in deep now," he told her. "I heard Macklin yell your name."

"It doesn't matter," she said. "What's it all about?"

"They've got me for everything under the sun," he said simply, and added, "Butch was right about that, anyway."

"Butch?"

"He's boss of the Wild Bunch. He said if he done everything they charged him with, he'd have to be six men. They've got me for that many, too. Hutchins thinks I robbed his bank and they all think I killed two men."

They rode in silence for a few minutes and then he burst out: "I deserve it for sticking my nose in a political squabble."

She didn't answer at once. Then she said, "They asked you, Logan. And I believe this can be worked out. Jerico will understand."

"My best bet is to go back to Butch," he said. "I'll never get around all this trouble stacked up in front of me."

"No," she said. "You know you wouldn't, Logan."

The thud of their horses' hoofs was the only sound in the night. Then he sighed. "I wish everybody thought like you."

"That'd be tiresome, too," she laughed. She noticed he'd changed direction. "Where're we going?"

"Back to town."

"Back to town! But Logan . . ."

"I got an idea," he said, and told her. The posse would be out beating the sage. They couldn't do much until morning, anyway. Then they might pick up sign. But even if they did, it'd give him time. "I need some time to talk to Jerico," he concluded.

She was still shaking her head when they reached town, still protesting. "They'll never give you a chance," she said wearily. "They'll shoot you through the bars of the jail. Or work up a necktie party."

"It's risky," he admitted. "But no more so than dodging around the prairie."

She gave in then. "Not quite daylight, but it soon will be. Maybe you can get into my room in the hotel. No one would think of looking there. At least not until Macklin gets back. And you said yourself he wouldn't be back in a hurry."

He put his hand on hers for a moment. "You're swell, Kathy," he said. Then gruffly added: "I'll put the horses away."

"No," she objected. "I'll turn them in the livery corral. You go right on up to my room. The door's unlocked."

"Just one thing," he said. "First chance you get see Gail and tell her everything's going to work out all right. Will you do it?"

She looked at him steadily for a long moment and then said, "Of course, Logan."

He watched her ride away, leading his horse. The street was dark and empty as he went up the wooden steps and peered through the window of the hotel lobby. It was deserted. That much he could see in the dim light of a smoky lamp. He went quietly across the porch and entered the doorway and stood there for a moment and then crossed the room and climbed the stairs.

He found her room and went in. He stood there in the darkness, and the room was warm with the fragrance of Kathleen, evoking images of her as she'd ridden with him tonight, and images of her all through the time he'd known her.

He waited, impatient for her return, and then he heard the soft fall of her footsteps and the door opened and she came into the room, bumping into him.

She said, "Oh," in a frightened voice, and then "Logan?"

"Don't worry," he said. "It's me all right."

Her sigh filled the room and she leaned against him, shivering. "I—I've become jumpy. Maybe I'm a sissy."

"You've been a swell little partner, Kathy."

For some reason she began sniffling and when Logan patted her shoulder she said crossly, "I'll get you a blanket. You can get some sleep on the floor. You probably need it."

She fetched him a blanket and a pillow and fixed a pad on the floor. He waited until she moved away and then lay down, staring into the darkness, hearing the small sounds of her movements and then the creak of the bed. He lay there listening to her breathing. It seemed to him that he'd known her forever. He achingly wished he'd known her before he met—he hastily thrust the disloyal thought from his mind.

He didn't think he could sleep. But miraculously, he dropped off.

CHAPTER EIGHTEEN

It was late morning when Kathleen Wisdom shook him awake. He rolled out of the blanket she'd given him and sat up yawning. She was dressed, appeared fresh and cheerful. She silently gave him a lard pail filled with steaming coffee.

"I didn't know if you liked milk and sugar," she said, "so it's black."

He yawned again and rubbed the black stubble on his face. "Either way," he said. He lifted the lard pail and sipped the coffee. It was hot and it was good.

"I was afraid to bring anything to eat," she said. "Someone might notice."

He nodded. "Thanks, anyway. Anything new?"

"The town's in an uproar," she said. "It's to be expected." She looked at him with appraising brown eyes. "I've some bad news."

He set the pail on the floor and drew up his feet and rested his elbows on his knees. "Like what?"

She gave him a ring, placing it in his hand. "Gail said—she said she didn't want to hear about it."

He dropped the ring in his shirt pocket and picked up the lard pail.

"I'm sorry, Logan," she said.

"That's all right, too," he said harshly, with the lard pail covering his face. "It's all right." He repeated the words slowly and distinctly.

She was quiet for a long moment, then she said, "Jerico wants to talk to you. He's waiting down in the lobby. Do you want to see him now?"

Logan set the lard pail on the floor and got to his feet. "Now's good a time as any," he said. He got his hat from beside the crumpled blanket and stood there with it in his hand. "I sure do thank you, Kathleen," he said.

"Maybe you'd better see him up here," she said, bright-eyed, too bright-eyed.

"No," he said. "It's all right now." He turned to the door and opened it. He didn't look back, because he was thinking that if things didn't go right, he might not see her again. He pulled the door shut. He didn't see Kathleen Wisdom put her face in her two hands. There was a wall and a closed door between them.

He went down the stairs and stopped at the landing, searching the lobby. The only occupant was Jerico Jones, sitting on the bullhide chair by the window. He turned his head and looked at Logan and stood up.

Logan came on down into the room.

Jerico surveyed him with his pale blue eyes. "Dang it, Logan," he said. "Somebody has played hell aplenty."

"I want to give myself up," Logan said.

Jerico squinted at him. "Kind of late for that," he said gruffly. "But there's nothing else for me to do. One thing, though—the judge and me talked it over and we decided the quicker the better. So you won't have long to wait, if that's any consolation."

"You don't think I'm guilty, do you?"

"T'aint what I think, Logan. It's the jury that will decide that."

Logan smiled wryly. "Then I'd better hope I got some friends on the jury."

"For what it's wuth," Jerico said, eying Logan speculatively, "I been doin' a little askin' around. You ain't entirely without friends." And he would say no more.

All the male population of Haymes County, it seemed to Logan, tried to crowd into the tiny courtroom that afternoon. They spilled out through the doorway and into the schoolyard, peering into the windows, jostling and pushing for a better view.

When Logan came in, manacled, Judge Benton was conferring at the bench with Kathleen Wisdom and Doc Custis. They terminated their conference as Logan was seated and Kathleen brushed by him without looking at him and took her seat at the place reserved for witnesses. With a slight shock, he saw that all the Candlish brothers except Duke were seated in the same section.

There was a buzz of voices as Jeb Candlish was called as a witness. The huge man shuffled up to the stand and was sworn. Under questioning by the county prosecutor—a thin, hawk-faced man named Obie Stevens—he established his identity and his place of residence. "Now then, Mr. Candlish," Stevens said, "in your own words tell the court what transpired last night, only those events you actually witnessed."

"I was just comin' out of the Longhorn," Candlish rumbled, "an' meanderin' around when I saw this light in the bank. 'Cause it's dark and bank's s'posed to be closed, I stopped and peeked in. There was Logan Marlowe and that little redheaded outlaw buddy o' his. I watched and they come out and the marshal—Logan, that is—climbed on his claybank and set there while that little redheaded feller run across the street to the newspaper office. I heard a shot, and then I noticed that Logan drove his claybank across the street and he had his pistol in his hand. He shot through the door and I saw Red drop like a rock."

Logan listened to this with amazement. He saw the Candlish brothers exchange glances in which there was thinly veiled triumph. He knew then that they were responsible for the death of his herd, that, now, they were trying to frame him for murder.

"You saw no one else on the street?" the prosecutor asked.

"That's right." Candlish nodded owlishly. "Is that all now?"

"Wait a minute, just a minute." Jerico Jones spoke as he rose. "There's a difference here that looks almighty suspicious."

Logan's heart set up a slow pound as he looked at the chains on his wrists and felt the helplessness come over him that had been lying underneath ever since he'd given himself up. He saw that Macklin's mouth was standing open and he swung his head.

Chet Morley, the blacksmith, came through the door, his broad shoulders filling the opening. He strode down the aisle, his powerful arms swinging, and went to the witness stand. Jeb Candlish, just as big but running to fat, stood aside for him.

After he was sworn to tell the truth, Chet rumbled, "I don't know nothin' about fancy questions and answers. I just heard Jeb from where I was standin' outside that door and I know he lied like a dog!"

There was a sudden hum in the courtroom and the judge pounded with his gavel, pounded the room into silence that made the fly on the windowpane audible.

Jeb moved over to the chairs occupied by his brothers and all over the room tension erupted as Jerico's men stood up here and there, watching the crowd, but mostly watching the Candlish men.

Chet Morley paid no attention to this byplay. He said, "How d' I know? Well, listen: Curly Jackson brought Logan's claybank up for me t' shoe. Matt Sandison come by just when I was gettin' ready t' shoe Logan's hoss and Matt wanted me to fix a busted wheel so's he could get back t' his ranch. I didn't get a chance to shoe Logan's horse, but I knowed Curly had some good hosses in his stable and I didn't worry about it. Now t' make a long story shorter, that claybank Candlish says he seen stayed in corral for nigh onto a week and I got a padlock on that corral gate that ain't been tampered with."

Jeb Candlish's bearded face was screwed into a tight mask of hate and he shouted, "He killed Duke, damn him! He killed Duke!" and pulled his gun.

Logan stood up and aside from the gun and brought the cuffs down on Candlish's head. The big man stumbled and fell and Logan fell on top of him. The courtroom was in an uproar and a gun went off in the back. Someone yelled, "Look out for Macklin!"

Al Macklin scrambled up on a table, looking over the heads of the surging, fear-maddened spectators clawing their way out of danger. On his knees beside Candlish, Logan grabbed the gun out of Candlish's hand and fired all in one motion. Macklin plunged headlong to the floor and his gun blasted again, triggered by a dying convulsion.

As though on a signal, everyone stopped pushing and shoving. Men looked at each other sheepishly, as they separated and stood, breathing noisily, suddenly loud-talking and trying to act unconcerned.

Jerico pushed his way through the crowd and helped Logan to his feet and took the gun from his hand, smiling at him.

"I guess I can unlock them cuffs, Logan boy," he

said, and turned his head to the still-pale prosecutor. "Shall I release the prisoner, Mister Stevens?"

Stevens blinked and shook his head. "There's a little matter of bank robbery . . ."

"I don't think you'll want to press that either," a new voice said from the rear of the room, and Kirk Hutchins stood up on a chair so that he could be seen. "I've got . . ."

"Kirk!" Glenn Hutchins roared. "You shut up, boy!" He took out a handkerchief and mopped his face. "Judge, your honor, sir, I wish to state here and now that I do not intend to press any charges against the accused."

The judge was smiling thinly. "Seems to me that there's something fishier than fish going on here, but I intend to entertain the prosecutor's motion for dismissal of all charges against Logan Marlowe."

"I so move," the prosecutor intoned.

"What's this about Logan bein' an outlaw?" someone in the crowd yelled.

Jerico stepped over Macklin's body and climbed up on the table where Macklin had stood a few moments before trying to get a shot at Logan. He held up his hands and got silence. "When Logan Marlowe became town constable I checked on him. He's clean. You got my word for it."

"That's good enough for me," Curly Jackson declared with a grin on his broad face, while Chet Morley nodded agreement.

"Me, too!" a chorus of voices welled up. They began to push toward the door again, but parted to let Kathleen Wisdom through. She came toward the group as Jeb Candlish sat up, with a trickle of blood running down his face. She stopped in front of Jeb and said, "You were wrong, Mr. Candlish, all wrong."

His eyes were still clouded and he shook his head. Kathleen glanced at Logan, saying, "He thought you killed his brother. Miss Howard told me that it was Al Macklin."

That got through to Candlish. He stared owlishly at Kathleen Wisdom and blinked his eyes. "I reckon you're some right. I see you're some smarter than Ben."

"Did you kill my brother?" she asked abruptly.

Jeb looked at Sheriff Jones. "You'd better take me out o' here," he rumbled.

Jerico nodded agreement. He sensed that this was something that could split the town wide. Lending credence to that sensing was the look on Glenn Hutchins' face as he pushed out the door, holding Kirk's arm. His special deputies had already hustled the Candlish twins away and now he nodded Jeb Candlish out, too. He pushed Logan away from the crowd and said, "I guess I should have told you long ago, boy."

"You knew about me?" Logan asked.

Jerico nodded. "Sure. Ever since you mailed the loot back. When the railroad got their money back and it was postmarked Haymes, they sent a Pinkerton man down. The Pinkerton man was all for taking you back, Logan. They wanted you to work for them. They claimed a man knowing as much about the Wild Bunch as you did, and goin' straight, could be real valuable."

Logan said, "Thanks," and looked around for Kathleen Wisdom, but she had left.

CHAPTER NINETEEN

Logan went from the newspaper office to the hote
and couldn't find Kathleen. He was continually be
ing stopped by people on the street and congratu
lated. He went down a side street and cut over to hi
boardinghouse and was met at the door by Alli
Adamson.

"Time you was getting back," she said severely. "
was just about to rent out your room."

"I'll bet," he said, scrubbing his hand across hi
face and feeling the bite of his unshaven face
"I could sure use some hot water."

"There's plenty on the stove," she said. "Th
tub's behind the stove and—well, you've lived her
a long time and I hope it'll be a sight longer."

"Thanks, Allie," he said, and went on into th
kitchen and slid the lock in place. He got out the bi
tin tub and filled it with hot water and strippe
down and stepped into the tub, his knees projectin

up almost to his chin. He took his bath unhurriedly and stepped out and dried off, and then stropped his razor and carefully shaved his face. There was clean clothing hanging across the chair and he dressed and cleaned up the kitchen and went out through the house and down toward the center of town. He made the rounds again, looking for Kathleen, but failed to find her.

At his own office he stopped on the porch and surveyed the street. Jerico Jones stepped out of the sheriff's office and motioned for him. He angled across the street, waited for a buckboard to pass and then stepped up beside Jerico.

"Come on in," Jerico said. "You may as well get the whole story now and get it over with."

They went into the musty office and Jerico sat at his desk and motioned for Logan to be seated.

"I'll stand," Logan said. "I'm still kind of jumpy."

Jerico nodded. "Jeb killed Ben Wisdom," he began. "Told me so hisself. Scared o' Ben, he was. Jeb never admitted it right out, but it's plain he was runnin' a hole-in-the-wall out on Snaketrack. Too many outlaws turned up on the dodge over there for it to be coincidence. But Jeb denied it. What he did tell was that Ben found out about his sheep deal and tried to blackmail him. Jeb wanted to keep it quiet about the sheep until he could point out to the cattlemen that his sheep wasn't gonna bother nobody. Ben put on the heat and Jeb shot him. That's when he dis-

covered the wanted poster on you. Ben was eve
throwin' that in."

"Does Kathleen know all this?"

Jerico nodded. "She knew the main points eve
before I did. Smart woman, that Wisdom gal."

"Well, anyway, Jeb heard she was comin' and ha
a couple of his owlhooters stop the train and try t
get her off. They didn't get her, as you know, and
guess the rest of it is pretty plain."

"All except one thing," Logan said. "I can't fin
Kathy."

"She's waitin'," Jerico said, "down at the statio
Gonna catch the next train east."

Logan felt a surge of panic. He went to the doo
and paused there. "I want to stop her," he said
"She's not guilty of anything."

"She's guilty of havin' Ben for a brother," Jeric
said.

"I've got to hurry," Logan said, hearing the thi
whistle of the train in the long distance. "There'
still some questions, Jerico . . ."

"All can be answered," Jerico said without smil
ing. He looked sad when he added, "We're all guilt
of something, Logan. Maybe Glenn did get Candlis
and Macklin to rob his bank. I can't prove it and I'
not tryin'. Maybe you can understand, maybe yo
can't, I don't know."

"But what about Merl Young and Red Bryson?"

"Candlish and Macklin did it. Macklin's dead an
Candlish blames everything on him. Maybe yo

don't understand this either, Logan, but I'm not pressing anyone anywhere." He turned his back on Logan and stalked to the window. "Go on," he said. "Stop that gal from leavin' this town."

Logan said, "Thanks," and walked out.

Giff Howard stood with his daughter in the shade of the hotel porch. They were both watching the sheriff's office and when Logan emerged they walked to meet him.

Logan stopped his impatient steps and waited. Gail came on to stand close to him, a smile on her face. She was a pretty girl, he thought, but that was just about it. "I had a grandstand seat at the trial, Logan. I saw it all through the window, sitting in my buggy. I'm glad everything turned out all right." She stood there expectantly, waiting, her small face tilted.

Besides her prettiness of face, he saw the sharpness of it and suddenly wondered what it was that had pulled him to her. She flushed at his gaze and her smile died as he said, "Thanks, Gail," and went on past her, meeting Giff's stiff gaze, saying, "It's all right, Giff. I'm not asking for your backing."

Giff Howard said gruffly, "I was a fool, boy. I'd like to have you in the family, o' course. But my backin' don't depend on nothin' but what I think o' you."

Impatience was still riding Logan hard. He said, "Thanks, Giff, and now I got to get to the station before the train gets in." He went past Giff, not looking back, and went with long strides toward the railroad station. He could see her standing on the platform and he fingered the ring in his pocket, wondering if she'd take a second-hand engagement ring. She turned then, and from the smile on her face, he thought she would.